"Why Am I Going To Chase You?"

Clovis wanted to know.

"To corrupt my morals," Sling replied.

"I see. Why am I going to do that?"

"Because you're curious about me, and you wonder if I'm a good lover."

"Why, Mr. Mueller! How you do go on! Have you been drinking?"

"No," he assured her. "I'm cold sober and very needy."

"You need . . . a drink?"

"A taste of you."

"How can you be so fresh?" she scolded. "We are barely acquainted."

"For now."

Dear Reader:

Welcome to Silhouette Desire! If you're a regular reader, you already know you're in for a treat. If this is your first Silhouette Desire, I predict you'll be hooked on romance, because these are sensuous, emotional love stories written by and for today's women—women just like *you!*

A Silhouette Desire can have many different moods and tones: some are humorous, others dramatic. But they *all* have a heroine you can identify with. She's busy, smart, and occasionally downright frazzled! She's always got something keeping her on the go: family, sometimes kids, maybe a job and there's that darned car that keeps breaking down! And of course, she's got that extra complication—the sexy, interesting man she's just met....

Speaking of sexy men, don't miss May's *Man of the Month* title, *Sweet on Jessie,* by Jackie Merritt. This man is just wonderful. Also, look for *Just Say Yes,* another terrific romance from the pen of Dixie Browning. Rounding out May are books by Lass Small, Rita Rainville, Cait London and Christine Rimmer. It's a great lineup, and naturally I hope you read them all.

So, until next month, happy reading!

Lucia Macro
Senior Editor

LASS
SMALL

NO TRESPASSING ALLOWED

SILHOUETTE *Desire*®

Published by Silhouette Books New York

America's Publisher of Contemporary Romance

SILHOUETTE BOOKS
300 East 42nd St., New York, N.Y. 10017

NO TRESPASSING ALLOWED

ISBN: 0-373-05638-9

First Silhouette Books printing May 1991

Printed in the U.S.A.

Books by Lass Small

Silhouette Romance

An Irritating Man #444
Snow Bird #521

Silhouette Desire

Tangled Web #241
To Meet Again #322
Stolen Day #341
Possibles #356
Intrusive Man #373
To Love Again #397
Blindman's Bluff #413
Goldilocks and the Behr #437
Hide and Seek #453
Red Rover #491
Odd Man Out #505
Tagged #534
Contact #548
Wrong Address, Right Place #569
Not Easy #578
The Loner #594
Four Dollars and Fifty-One Cents #613
No Trespassing Allowed #638

Silhouette Books

Silhouette Christmas Stories 1989
"Voice of the Turtles"

LASS SMALL

finds that living on this planet at this time is a fascinating experience. People are amazing. She thinks that to be a teller of tales of people, places and things is absolutely marvelous.

One

———

When it was time to fill in the grave at the county cemetery, the custodian made Sling Mueller wait until the handful of dutiful townspeople had driven away. Nobody could label any of them as mourners, because who'd mourn for that old biddy?

With the pickups leaving, Tim leaned on his shovel and allowed the volunteers to fill the grave.

Sling mentioned to Colin, "We ought to've put a wooden stake through her heart."

The men smothered their laughter.

Sling went on: "When I get done here, I'm going over and pull down that house. I don't want anybody else moving in there."

Ham-handed and bulky, Colin Kilgallon handled the shovel like a child's toy. "You're gonna miss that old lady."

"About like I'd miss a continuous case of hives," Sling corrected. "Here on out, I'm going to breathe free."

"Did you ever once think she might have been a side dish for your great granddaddy?"

Sling slung in another shovelful of dirt. "Surely the old man had better taste than that."

"He allowed her to live in the house," Colin reminded Sling. "So did your granddaddy and your daddy. You did, too."

"It was charity. From what I hear tell, my great-granddaddy was a pushover. You've all heard that. But he wouldn't've touched Lizzie with a ten-foot pole."

"I hadn't heard he was that well endowed." Tim chortled.

"Now, now," Ned scolded.

"I was some surprised to find her real name was Eileen." Phillip Joe mentioned that. "Interesting she was called Lizzie."

Sling was positive. "She was called after the woman who took an ax and hit her daddy forty whacks."

Colin said rather pensively, "She must have blossomed into a sticker burr early. I never heard her called Eileen in all my days. I wonder how the preacher found out that name for Lizzie. Maybe we buried somebody else?"

Sling shook his head emphatically. "Naw, it's her. I checked to be sure we got the right one. I'd hate for the old lady to come around, climb out of her casket and move back into that house."

Colin eyed Sling. "I've never heard you complain before this."

"What good would it've done? She was my responsibility. But she never let up. If it wasn't one thing, it was another. All my days, anytime, day or night. Telephones are a curse to mankind."

Ned soothed Sling. "She knew she could count on you."

"She was a millstone around my neck. I'm glad to be shed of her."

"You were a good neighbor, Sling," Ned said. "A kinsman couldn't have been more kind to a lone woman."

"I get no credit. I had no choice." Sling grumbled the words. Then he said, "Hey, Tim, when you set the gravestone, how about putting it in the middle of the plot? That might keep her down."

"Naw. If I put it in the middle, it'd upset the symmetry of the other stones."

That surprised the whole lot of them. They exchanged an amazed look.

Sling said positively, "Nobody has ever come out here to eye the lineup of the stones. Nobody would even notice. They're all helter-skelter. Look at them! And nobody is going to be putting flowers on this harpy's grave, so who'd know?"

"I run a tidy graveyard," Tim said firmly. He also ran the only motel in that area near to Kerrville, Texas. The motel was rackety. That aspect of the place was seldom noticed by the kind of clients he had.

Ned asked, "How come there aren't any cockroaches out here when your motel is overrun with them?" That was a common question.

Tim's reply was automatic and familiar. "These folks don't eat in bed."

It always brought a laugh.

Done with their task, they rounded off the covering dirt and put the few garden flowers on the grave. They took off their hats and stood for the required minute of silence.

Then Sling said, "So long, Lizzie Wilson. I never dreamed you'd last this long."

"They never found no kin?" Colin paused as he questioned that.

"They probably all hid." Sling was sure. "If you guys want to do me a favor, meet me tomorrow at the house and help me empty it out and tear it down."

As they gave versions of agreement, they walked to their pickups, put their shovels in the back ends, said goodbye and separated as they went off in different directions.

Sling drove away, thinking about Lizzie. That old lady had lived on a corner of the Mueller land all his life, and she had felt the Muellers were responsible for her comfort and security and errands. She'd never even once said "Thank you."

To hear her tell it, they were either too long doing whatever it was, or they'd brought the wrong kind or not enough. She'd been a real pain.

When Sling's parents had died, long ago, he'd inherited not only the responsibility of the land and his younger brothers and sisters but old Lizzie, as well.

As of today, Sling was alone. He had no one else who depended on him or had first call on him. Sling Mueller was free of all the obligations his parents had loaded on his young shoulders fifteen years before.

He was thirty-four years old and debt free for the first time in his life. The Mueller children had worked their tails off to get themselves to this point. They were all educated, established and acquiring new debts.

Sling knew he would never marry. He didn't want to get back into the trap of being responsible for anyone. If he married, the woman would probably want kids, and he'd be right back on the treadmill.

And sure as he was sitting there in his new pickup, the woman would have an aging mother who needed errands, care, or whose house needed repairs. There was no way at all that he'd be sucked into anything like that again.

He didn't need anybody underfoot. The sparse community was a friendly one, and Sling had plenty of companionship when he felt the need. There were parties. There were friendly women who wanted commitment as little as he. He was free.

So. That night he should have had a full night's sleep, but he wakened and listened several impatient times. He gradually understood that it would take a while for him to become accustomed to being free of all the pressures he'd coped with for so long.

When Sling wakened in the morning, it was earlier than he needed to be up. But he rose, puttered around, made some coffee, looked out at the streaking sunrise and listened to the silence.

He was tall and lanky, a beautifully made man with no hips, a flat stomach and the wide, strong shoulders of a man who did physical work. He was every woman's dream of a highwayman: dark and dangerous looking.

He dressed in a cotton, long-sleeved blue shirt, automatically tied a cotton kerchief around his neck, then pulled on jeans, socks and boots.

He went outside and fed his hound. It was a liver-spotted hunting dog named...Spots. After that, Sling ate his own breakfast without thinking about what he ate, and he was finished without him knowing what he'd had. He left the dishes in the sink for Chin, the cook.

Carrying his jacket, he went restlessly out on his porch. The July morning was cool. He pulled on a jean jacket, settled his Stetson on his head, whistled for Spots and went out to his truck.

He drove to the house Lizzie had vacated. It had originally been built as a grandparents' house. Those were set separately from the main place on land that was handed down to the next generation. When the kids were grown, the parents moved into the smaller house, relinquishing the larger one to the growing family of the eldest son.

Sling would never live in the grandparents' house. He would never marry; there would be no children; he would only give up the Home Place when he died. Then his next oldest brother would figure out what the family was to do with the land.

He smiled at his pickup. His first new one. He rather missed the old one with the rattles and squeaks that warned of need. This truck rode smooth and silent, and the motor's muted roar sounded of power. Next, he'd buy a car. A muscle machine. That was what he would do.

He got to the doomed house that no longer held that hellion, Lizzie Wilson, and he smiled. It again belonged to the Muellers. He was going to pull it down.

Lizzie had had the two great oaks near the house sawed down and cut up. Trees were precious in Texas. Those oaks had been three hundred years old. And old Lizzie had destroyed them. He'd raised hell over that, but she'd wanted a clear view of—nothing.

Sling looked around. There was an empty creek bed about two hundred feet over. Along the waterway, there were scrub mesquites with their scrawny trunks and lacy leaves. There were some cottonwoods, and on down the wash, out of Lizzie's reach, was a surviving large, beautiful oak.

Sling got out of his truck and stood in the yard. The dog jumped down and went ranging off. Looking around, Sling saw that the weeds needed mowing. They could just go on and grow. He wasn't cutting them ever again.

Then he turned and looked at the two-story, sparse and angular box of a house, sitting up off the ground on posts. The porch was roofless, but it went all the way around the house like a railed deck, and the roof was flat with a railing around it.

There wasn't any visible paint left on any of the bare boards. Until now, there hadn't been the money for it.

God, how he missed his parents. Still.

And yet again, Sling wondered why his great-grandfather had allowed Lizzie to take over the house and why she'd been allowed to stay there ever since.

He went inside and the place smelled like Lizzie. Stale. Sour. He opened windows and doors, before he carried the mattress and bedding outside to be pitched.

He looked at the rest of the furniture and noted all that was there. He checked for their family-furniture brand, and it appeared on most of the good pieces. ling carried and dragged those pieces out to the tacky yard to be hauled back home.

Getting the chain from his pickup, he ran it under the house to the center post and he took a grim pleasure in doing that. He attached the other end to his pickup's axle. It would only take a tug to have the whole tinderbox of dry boards come tumbling down.

He was tempted to just go ahead and do that because it would be so satisfying, but he'd promised the other gravediggers a share in the treat.

He slouched against his truck and surveyed the prospective ruin. He watched Spots investigating along the dry creek bed. Then he looked at the Texas sky and listened to the birdsongs as the Gulf breeze teased him, cooling him.

Colin was the first there. He drove up in his own pickup and got out slowly, looking around. "Moving?"

"How do you suppose that old woman got all that stuff over here from the Home Place? Every single one of those pieces has our household brand on it."

"Lizzie didn't have a pickup. Somebody had to've brought those things over here."

"I can't believe either my grandmother or mother agreeing to Lizzie having those family things. It just does not make sense."

Colin didn't have an answer to that. "Kyle said he wants to see this, too, and you're not to move a beam until he gets here. We've all got bets on what it'll take to get the place trashed. You want to sell the kindling? There's a couple of offers.'' Colin pulled some papers from his shirt pocket.

"Whoever clears it away can have the splinters and boards free and clear.''

"Don't be in such a hurry when you can make a nickel or two. These bids include carting the stuff away. One will even drag a magnet for—get this—the odd nails. I asked about the *even* nails, but they just looked patient and wouldn't discuss that.''

"Here they come. Now we get to do it. Sorry I interrupted, Pig.''

And Colin laughed at the old nickname.

The other pickups turned in and parked on the weeds away from Sling and Colin. Sling said to Colin, "Maybe you ought to pull your truck over there by theirs. That house could skid in the falling.''

"Good thinking.''

"It's just a good thing you waited for us.'' Ned got out of his truck.

"What kept you guys?'' Sling asked.

"We do have obligations at home, you got to remember,'' Phillip Joe mentioned. "We aren't unfettered like some. You guys must have been up with the roosters this morning.''

Tim was still dubious. "You're really going to do this thing? The house is in prime condition. Seems a real shame.''

The rest hooted, and Sling said, "With the condition of your motel, I can see how you'd not recognize it's a dilapidated shack.''

But Colin got pensive. "It does seem a shame. That old house has stood here . . . how long?''

Sling looked at it as he calculated. "Over ninety years, closer to a hundred. It's time to take it down. It's a firetrap. The boards are tinder."

A car slowed, hesitated and crept along the fence line. It was a sassy white sports car that looked like money, and that had the men's attention.

Because the rising sun was so bright behind the driver, the men could only see the silhouette of a woman's head and shoulders. She had to be young to wear her hair so free. It looked luxuriant, soft and inviting to a man's hands.

They squinted and moved their heads to try to see her features. And since she appeared to be staring at them, some of the men moved in the way of men who are conscious that a woman is watching, but Sling only frowned at the car.

Using the panel control, the woman lowered the passenger-side window and called, "What are you trying to do?"

Her voice was delicious. It slid down in parched areas of the men's souls and their faces softened. All but Sling's.

Phillip Joe called back, making his voice lower, "We're tearing down this old dilapidated house."

She closed the window and drove away.

Ted asked, "How come you didn't invite her to watch?"

"I never had the chance."

"Wonder what she looks like. Her voice..."

"Who was that?" Phillip Joe watched after the car.

Tim took his Stetson and raised it in order to tilt the brim against the early sun so that he could watch after the car. "Not local."

"Civilization's getting so close that too many strangers are prowling around," Sling groused. "Too often, nowadays, all sorts of cars go around just like they have the right to go through here."

"Let's get this done," Ted urged. "I've brought my camera. I'm going to tape the great housewrecking and sell the copies. I'll make my fortune, leave this land and go live in San Antonio on the river."

Phillip Joe urged, "Let's get to it. Got all the stuff out?"

"All that's ours," Sling said. "You guys are free to go in and take what you want."

"You made a haul," Tim said.

"All family stuff. I don't know how the old biddy got all this stuff away from my grandmother or my mother. Somebody wasn't paying attention."

Again Ted said, "Let's go. Hustle up, you guys. Get what you want."

Phillip Joe came out with the parts of a bedstead. "You sure you don't want this, Sling?"

"Positive."

Each of the men found at least one thing that he felt made the trip worthwhile. They were pleased with the freebies, which they put into the trucks. And finally they straightened the chain, and Sling got into his pickup. "Okay?" he yelled. "Everybody out of the way? The chain could snap or the house could shatter and scatter. Get close to some kind of shield. Durned woman had a crew cut down all the trees."

The men calculated the house with narrowed eyes and moved back a ways. Then they called, "All clear!"

Sling revved the motor to trembling and then let off the brake and the vehicle bucked. The motor roared and strained, but the house stood firm.

The watchers rose from their braced, crouched positions and watched as they relaxed.

With the smell of burned rubber, Sling let up on the gas pedal. Then, as the motor idled in the silence, he turned off the key.

Sling got out of the truck, pushed back his Stetson and stood with his hands on his hips as he surveyed the damned stubborn house.

"Wow!" said Tim. "Do you know how many horsepower that truck has? And it didn't budge that flimsy old house. What's the matter?"

Colin replied, "Houses are supposed to be wrecked by cranes and bulldozers. Pickups are for hauling."

Sling sighed. "Who would ever believe that house would stay put?"

"Let's add my truck to yours," Colin suggested.

So they did that. They laid the chains carefully straight and everyone else moved to safety. Colin had gotten into his pickup and Sling was about to get into his, when the sheriff's car came down the road with flashing lights and shrieking siren. He was followed by the white car that had passed by the house earlier.

Sling closed his truck door, and Colin opened his door and got out. Curious, the men watched.

The sheriff turned into that lane! He pulled up onto the weeds in front of Sling's pickup as if to block it, and he got out rather ponderously official. He returned their nods but didn't say anything.

The gathered men waited.

And the other car eased onto the weeds just the other side of their group. In it was the woman.

The men stared, fascinated, as she opened her sassy little white car's door and put out a foot that wore a very high heel. She was careless of her skirt. Watching, the men immediately realized—even Phillip Joe knew—that she wasn't being flauntingly careless. She was oblivious to them as men. How insulting for any woman to do that to a bunch of men.

But each, knowing that he was superior if for no other reason than that he was Texan, did watch her quite avidly.

She stood up straight and prim but her blond hair was teased by the wind. So were her skirts, and she was such a sight that the men didn't know where to look.

She wasn't a tall woman, but she was lithe and moved beautifully. She slammed the car door and her firm, round, braless breasts jiggled individually. She looked at the house, then she said to the sheriff, "Arrest them."

"Now, honey—"

"Miss Culpepper," she corrected.

"Ye—"

Sling asked, "You part of the San Antonio Culpeppers?"

She looked at him silencingly and said to the sheriff, "Arrest him. He's the one who carried out the furniture."

"Hon—uh. That's the man who owns this place?" He questioned with the statement in a do-you-understand manner.

"My cousin lived here for sixty-seven years. She owned it. It's mine. Get these men to take that furniture back inside where it belongs and get them off my land.''

Other than the sheriff, the men all burst out laughing.

She was not amused.

The sheriff said, ''Boys, this is serious. She has papers.''

''On what?'' Sling wanted to know.

''On this land.''

''Great-grandpa *gave* it to Lizzie?''

''No. But you all let her live here.'' The sheriff pointed out that obvious thing to them.

''That's right,'' Sling agreed. ''She had no place to go.'' He looked at Miss Culpepper. ''And in all those years, no one ever showed any interest in Lizzie. We look care of her all her days. We even buried her.''

Miss Culpepper said, ''Thank you.''

''Now you just tell me how sad you are that the old woman's dead.'' Sling gave her a very nasty look.

''I never met her.''

''Then how come you come roaring in here with the sheriff, honey? You just read about the death in the papers? And you're the first of a flight of hungry buzzards?''

''No. Apparently I'm a distant cousin. She has left me this house.''

''And you arrive the day after she's buried? How did you find out? Carrier pigeon? I hate to disappoint you, but I own this place. It's on my land. I've put up with that harridan all my life, and I'll be damned if I'll tolerate another of her breed coming to roost here on my land.''

''It's legal.''

"So, on occasion, are murder and dismemberment." Sling's voice was unkind. "Who says your claim is legal?" Sling's manner made the men nervous because they could never remember his tone being so deadly. Nobody pushed Sling. Miss Culpepper was being unpardonably reckless. Careless.

"I have the papers."

"Where?" He looked down her dismissively. Any other woman would have wilted in despair or at least flinched under such a scornful glance.

"I haven't yet copied the papers, and I would be a fool to give you the only copies."

He nodded. "Cautious. You have reason for caution? Your bid a little shaky?"

"No. It's solid."

"Honey—" the expression was not a term of endearment "—the Muellers have owned this land since before Mexico claimed it. We bought it from the Indians and have lived here continuously. You have no claim. This is my land and my house. And I choose to pull it down. That'll solve your little claim."

"No!" she said sharply.

"Hold it," said the sheriff. "She does have papers. I seen them. This—" he gestured to the house "—will have to wait until it's settled in court."

"I have a lawyer who'll say she doesn't get a dime." But he figured he would never need to consult one.

"It'll have to be decided." The sheriff was firm.

"A damned buzzard comes in on me and makes me prove what we've had for almost four hundred years is mine? We bought it, paid for it and have lived on it all this time. What a sneaky little bitch you are. I'll bet you *are* kin to that woman. She was just like you. All that furniture? Every piece out here has the Mueller household brand on it. We've run into thieves before, and we've learned to protect ourselves."

The men were fascinated. They'd never seen Sling riled. Nothing had ever made him get his back up this way. *And he was being rude to a lady!* He had to be the first of his whole family who'd ever been forced to do that. He was probably very embarrassed. Or maybe he didn't yet realize that he was dealing with a lady. They looked at Miss Culpepper. He could not miss the fact that she was female.

She was standing up to him. He didn't intimidate her one bit. Now, that was a surprise. Along with being rash, she must be just plain stupid.

Sling said in a mean voice, "It's very strange Lizzie never mentioned you."

And she said right back, "In the papers, she mentioned you." She gave him her own scathingly dismissive glance and said tellingly, "Not all of it was bad."

Two

The men chortled to hear any lady speak unkindly to Sling. Around him, women tended to purr and flirt and smile. Now Miss Culpepper had said old Lizzie hadn't spoken nicely about Sling. After all he'd done for the old biddy, she'd bad-mouthed him?

Sling gave Miss Culpepper a slow, rejecting look and said, "Had you bothered to know your kinswoman, you would consider the source."

The sheriff said, "Now, Sling, let's be gentlemanly about this. Miss Culpepper has no place to go. Let her just stay here until this thing is straightened out. Okay?"

Sling shoved his hands into his pockets and took a deep breath to blast the sheriff right on over into the next county—

And Colin said, "That's not unreasonable."

Sling looked at Colin as if he'd turned red and grown horns and a tail.

Phillip Joe smiled at Miss Culpepper and agreed. "Just for a time."

"No harm in that," Kyle put in.

And Tim said, "Where're your things? We could help you move in."

Tim was asking *permission* to help her move into the Mueller house. Sling protested: "She gets settled in there, and I'll never get her out. The Muellers have had a long experience with this woman's admitted kin. Did she ever help Lizzie?"

"Eileen," Miss Culpepper corrected.

"Had you known her, you would be aware that she has been called Lizzie all this time."

"I wonder why?"

"Probably because she chopped up somebody," Sling said nastily to the woman.

The sheriff placated them. "Now, now. Nothing comes of quarreling."

Sling said, "I'm not quarreling. I'm giving evidence that this woman didn't know Lizzie, doesn't know the facts, and I'm trying to avoid another bloodsucker from moving in on us."

Miss Culpepper turned to the sheriff, one hand holding her breeze-tousled hair from her face as she looked at the man loftily and asked for clarification. "This is the man? This man is Sling Mueller?"

"Yes, ma'am."

"He isn't at all the way you represented him."

The sheriff shrugged. "I guess he finally felt he was free of Lizzie. She was a trial to him."

"How much bother could an old lady be?" She lifted her chin as she looked back at Sling.

He turned and braced both hands on his pickup. The men knew he was expending anger by pushing on the truck. That awed them. He'd not only talked mean to a lady and called her a bitch to her face, but he was mad enough to need to expend his temper by pushing on a truck. They watched avidly.

Colin said to Miss Culpepper, "Any of these pieces you could need? You might go into the house and look around?" He used the questioning statement to ask if she'd care to do that. "We'll unload our trucks and you can look the stuff over and see what you want to use. Sling will lend you the Mueller things until you can replace them."

"*I did not say that she—*"

Colin just continued: "Let's go see what's left and what you'll need."

"Why, there is a gentleman here." She sounded surprised.

So the rest of the damned fools had to be helpful and prove they, too, were gentlemen. She allowed them to aid her. She never cast even a snide look over to the smoldering Sling.

Sling watched in a temper, and the sheriff stood by to wrestle Sling to the ground—if that was needed, and if he could do it. Hoping not to be tested, he sweat a little in the cooling Gulf breeze.

Busily the rest of the men accompanied Miss Culpepper into Sling's house. He could hear them as they went from room to room and discussed what would be needed.

Then, singly or in pairs, they came outside, ignoring Sling, and selected what she requested of the furniture in the yard. They did do that. It was *his* furniture, and they simply gave her what she wanted. It took forever.

Sling couldn't decide if he should go inside, or if that would be conceding defeat. He decided he wouldn't budge. Or maybe he'd go home and call his lawyer.

She came out finally and actually came to Sling. His damned dog went over, wagging his silly whip of a tail and stretched up his head to call attention to the fact that he would allow her to pet him. She did.

Her breasts shimmered with her movements and the wind loved teasing in her hair and blowing up her skirts. Sling kept his eyes grimly on her face. She had brown eyes with that blond hair.

To Sling, she said formally, "Thank you for allowing me to use the furniture that belonged to my cousin. Obviously, it was brought here—to her—for her use. I concede that those . . . branded pieces should be returned to you. I understand you have siblings who have their own homes and could use some of the heirloom pieces. Did they manage to escape from your control?" She tacked that on with a sweet smile.

He gave her a hard look and replied, "Yes."

"Good for them."

"Now, wait a minute," the sheriff began an appalled protest, but Sling silenced him with a glance. Sling had *never* silenced anyone with a real rude glance that way, and that was what silenced the sheriff. Shock.

Miss Culpepper turned and went back into the house, walking over the rough ground on those high heels with perfect precision. Not once did she falter or stumble.

She already had all that tribe of men eating from her hand. They were busily running around, working up a sweat, doing as she asked. She was being so sweet to them that sugar wouldn't have melted in her mouth.

He watched her laugh, and he listened as the men all laughed indulgently. It galled Sling. These men were *his* friends?

He put the rejected pieces of furniture into the back of his pickup. The sheriff tried to help, but he was a little too round and he puffed alarmingly. Sling unkindly snarled to him: "Cut it out."

After that, the sheriff just watched. He knew better than to go inside and help Miss Culpepper, but he watched and listened to the goings-on inside the house like a neglected waif. He was disgusting.

When Sling's truck was loaded and Sling had called his dog off the porch to the pickup, Colin came out and asked, "Leaving?"

"I wasn't invited to the...party." He ground down on that last word.

And Colin laughed.

Sling got into his truck and shoved the dog over. Colin came around to the driver's side and put his hands on the open windowsill. "Come to dinner tonight."

Sling looked at his longtime friend and said coldly, "I'll see."

Colin nodded, amused, and lifted his hands to put them back on the sill in a pat, before he dropped them

to his sides and stepped back. Then Colin had the guts
to say, "It'll be okay."

Sling drove back to his place, and the ranch hands
were there. They smiled and greeted him and the dog
kindly, and helped unload the furniture to carry it up
to the attic of the house.

As they made the trips in and out of the house, Sling
could see that the men hadn't been loafing. Chores
had been completed. The men on the place were good
and willing workers.

Most of the herds had been sold off, and with the
income from the last two bumper years, all Sling's
debts were paid and money had been put aside for the
next two years' taxes.

Sling had declared a semisabbatical for the ranch,
and now the ground would lie fallow for that time.
And during this while, he would be paying regular
wages and encouraging the men to take time and see
something of the world. They'd set up schedules so
that there were always sufficient hands around to keep
the place tidy and mended.

He'd been paying them enough already, but he'd
made such a killing in the herd sales that he'd shared
it. The men had been so startled, he'd had to warn
them that if the year busted, so would the raise. They
were still exuberant, and he'd figured he'd ruined a
good bunch of hands. But he found they were eager to
do their share, and that attitude hadn't faltered.

After the repossessed furniture had all been stored
safely in the attic, Sling discovered—quite by acci-
dent—that if he crouched down by the slotted wooden
air vent and pressed his face against the slats hard

enough, he could see past the rise to her hou—the Mueller grandparents' house.

It appeared to Sling that all the pickups were still there. What were they doing all this while? How much rearranging had to be done with the purloined Mueller furniture? Maybe the boys were spring-cleaning the house for her? Fredricka would have a fit if Colin was spending time that way, with a brown-eyed blonde.

And Sling thought it might be a good idea to just drop by Colin's place and mention that to Fredricka. What excuse could he have for going past Colin's place after just seeing him?

Sling thought he could say, "Oh, isn't Colin back yet? I'd have thought they would be finished moving *her* furniture by now."

Fredricka had an unexpected streak of curiosity. She'd ask who the "her" was.

Sling couldn't do it.

Although he did rack his brain as he paced in the attic, Sling couldn't think of one thing that he could use as any reason at all to stop off and tattle to Fredricka. Not that Colin would be annoyed; he'd find Sling's conduct hilarious.

So Sling stayed home.

He went around messing with equipment that didn't need attention. When he realized that, he understood that he was still mad at that woman for moving into his house, on his land. How was he going to evict her when the sheriff was on her side?

It would be revealing to see the papers that Miss Culpepper said proved her ownership. Anyone else own Mueller land? No way.

Was she a real blonde? It would be interesting to find out. Brown eyes were rare in a true blonde. He really didn't give a damn if she was or wasn't.

With his eye straining around the slats' meager view, he remembered that Miss Culpepper had a very nice body. Long legs. He would have liked to be the wind teasing around that woman. Yes.

The thing was, a wind could leave. A man would have to listen and adjust. And so far, Sling hadn't found any woman worth all that trouble.

Tom came in the door below and yelled up: "Lunch is ready. You interested?"

Sourly, Sling replied, "Yeah." He went down the attic stairs.

Tom went on: "The heat wave's on the way. They predict a wind chill of one hundred five."

Summers in Texas, the "wind chill" reports were a joke. It took all kinds of people to make the right mix. Sling was tolerant of weather reports. Then he thought: Good. Let it get hot like that and she won't be able to stand it.

"The cook's ailing. Jack took him in to the doctor. Want to go into town with us for supper?"

"Might."

Tom said, "We'll be taking off about five. Thought we'd go over to Fredericksburg and have a German meal. Okay?"

"I'll see, closer to time."

"Good enough." Tom was a cheerful soul. A young roustabout, he could ride anything, but he preferred women. The trouble was, they kept coming out to the ranch to see him. The other men were envious because Tom wouldn't share.

Sling asked, "What's the matter with Chin?"

"He fainted."

Sling frowned, got up, took his Stetson and went outside. Tom trailed along. "When did they go?" Sling asked.

"'bout two hours ago."

The liver-spotted dog rose eagerly, but Sling said, "Stay." Then he told Tom, "I think I'll go in and see what's going on with him. Thanks, Tom. Give me a rain check on the invite to supper."

"Sure."

Sling frowned back at Tom. "You guys behave, now, hear?"

"Pure as the driven snow," Tom promised in the face of a predicted scorcher.

Sling wondered how could a battered man look that innocent. Especially since Sling knew Tom surely wasn't.

Sling got into his pickup and departed. He now had the reason to drop by Colin's place.

Colin's wife Fredricka came out on the porch as Sling stopped his truck under a pecan tree at the edge of their graveled driveway's parking area. Having such a parking area proved they had lots of company. Sling inquired, "Colin still not home?"

Smiling casually at their lifelong friend, Fredricka said, "I thought he was with you. Did you pull down that house? It would be a shame to demolish it. Or did you get smart and change your mind?"

He frowned at Fredricka. She'd always been so docile, but in the past year she'd gotten feisty. She'd been shameless during last May's Homecoming, and just before the closing fireworks, she'd made no bones about marking Colin as her own. Some women were bold. Sling felt he'd been lucky never to have attracted Fredricka's attention.

A little testy, Sling replied, "When Colin comes back, tell him I've gone into town, that Chin fainted. They took him in to the doctor." He started back to his pickup, then turned and said sourly, "Your husband just might have an interesting tale to tell."

"Good. Bring back some shrimp if there's any at the store?"

"I'm not going to the store." He got into his pickup and left.

Testy. Hmmm. What a wonder. Sling had not only declined an errand, and that was past all good manners, but old easygoing Sling hadn't said "Hello" or "Goodbye." Fredricka shaded her eyes with her hand and looked off in the direction of the road, but only Sling's dust hung in sight. Thoughtfully, she went back to her drawing board.

At the doctor's office, Sling found Chin had been taken to the hospital.

So he hurried over there. With consolidated schools a fact, the hospitals had been next to combine. That way, they had better equipment and a better staff. Like the high school, the hospital was set off in the middle of nowhere.

Inside, Sling inquired about his cook. Information said it looked as if Chin had ptomaine poisoning!

With the word, Sling felt queasy. "Ptomaine? You're joshing."

"Cut it out," the old biddy on the desk growled. "There's no reason to joke about this. He's really sick."

"He's our cook!"

That caught her attention. "Oh? How're the rest of you?"

"I'm not too sure."

"You're a little pale." She eyed him like a vulture on a tree limb looking down at a dying rabbit.

Sling backed away. "I'm Sling Mueller. I pick up Chin's tab. Call me if he needs me."

"You're Sling?" She narrowed her eyes as she weighed him. "I've heard about you. A lady-killer."

"I am not!"

"You got the reputation." She was firm and a little critical.

Sling frowned darkly. He looked like a smolderingly wicked man that any smart woman would avoid.

The old biddy smiled. "I have a niece that you might take to—"

"Sorry." And he walked away, deliberately thudding his boots on the carpet runner. He went out, got into his pickup and drove away toward home.

Since he'd always seemed to attract female attention, he'd long ago found that the best defense was to escort an uninteresting, uninterested woman.

He'd used Fredricka Lambert for years as a safe partner. She'd been unthreatening, quiet, pretty enough, and she hadn't clung to him. Then, too, she'd gone off to Africa for six years, and everyone had thought he was waiting for her to come home. When she did, they went places together just like always, but then she'd up and married Colin Kilgallon a couple of months ago. That had annoyed Sling.

Her getting married to Colin had left Sling vulnerable, fair game to salivating females bent on nailing him into the early coffin of matrimony. He didn't need that. He had always had a couple of friendly female friends, but they didn't go around in the crowds where Sling was invited, so they were no shield.

After Fredricka had snared a very willing Colin, women had realized Sling was loose and he had been badgered by them. Not only had unattached women tried to pair up with him, but other people had pestered him to go places.

No matter where he went, Sling knew there would always be women at those places who didn't like being single. With him being loose, those women would think he was free for the picking. More and more, in these past few months, he went out less and less, even to crowded gatherings.

With his escape from the hospital receptionist and the proffered niece, Sling realized that he could slowly turn into a recluse. It was a sorry state of affairs when a man had to retreat like that just to protect himself. What about a man's inalienable rights? Man's liberation?

He'd finally gotten his life under control, and now here came some strange woman who was claiming a corner of his land. Figure that.

His own brothers would listen to that woman and be impartial. They were the New Men who did housework and changed babies and all that stuff.

Well, of course, while they were young, they'd *had* to help out in the house and with each other while they'd all struggled to last through that trying time. But it was no excuse, now, for them to go into the Twilight Zone of gender just because their wives worked. Women ought to stay home.

Even that wimpy Fredricka was up to her neck in a design business of her own. Who would ever have guessed that Colin Kilgallon would be so proud of his wife making her own money? Colin! Such conduct just didn't fit a ham-handed, red-headed man like him.

If things went on as they were going, Sling Mueller would be the last true male of his generation in the area. It was a sobering thought.

The rumble of thunder distracted Sling from his plight. He looked to the western sky that roiled with heavy clouds. That was how he felt, just like those clouds. He watched them sourly. They'd be lucky to get a sprinkle. With everything wet, and the sun back out, the heat wave would be muggy and awful.

He thought of that woman, Miss Culpepper, who was living on his land in a leaky house that had no air-conditioning. Sling Mueller smiled.

Old Lizzie had raised hell with Sling the last time it had rained. That had been some time back, and he had promised to fix the roof. It might well leak on this occasion. His laugh was a little dirty. That woman living on his land would have a fit, that Miss Culpepper. She would move out when she found that roof leaked.

And with his effort to destroy the center pole just that morning, it might even leak worse! Hah!

It rained so that Sling's pickup was almost clean by the time he arrived home. He got out and stood still, letting his Stetson brim protect his eyes as he watched the curtain of mist.

It really was beautiful. The rain-grayed, washed colors were so subtle. The unpainted woods darkened as they soaked up the moisture. And the dusty greens brightened.

Miss Culpepper would get soaked.

But then the rain stopped. Even as Sling watched, the clouds parted and some blue showed in the gray and black.

Sling turned to go into the house, and he saw that what moisture there was had only been enough to bead on the dust. Well, Texas was a big state. It took a lot of everything just to make do.

He went up to the attic without really thinking about what he was doing, and strained his eyes around the corner of the slotted attic opening. *She was covering the roof with a tarp.* And there were men busily helping her! *Who were they?* He was going to make a list.

Sling started across the attic on his way to drive past her house—*his* house!—and saw the old telescope. His dad had gotten that a long time ago. Sling had never had the time to be interested in stars, except for those needed to guide a man at night. And there'd never been any close neighbors to watch—until now.

He got out the hammer, removed the damned slotted wooden vent cover and adjusted the telescope. It was like being there. There was Colin! Did Fredricka know about Colin being there with that lascivious Miss Culpepper?

And there was Fredricka! What the hell was a woman doing over there helping out that siren? Anybody'd think—

There was Fredricka's mother, Ethel Lambert! And Ethel's best friend, Natalie Comstock! Good gravy.

That Miss Culpepper had the two most socially powerful women in the area helping her pull a tarp over the leaking roof. That was outside of too much.

Sling slumped down against the wall, but he adjusted the telescope so that he could keep watch.

And his mind worked.

If he was going to keep that house and get rid of Miss Culpepper, he was going to have to do something to thwart her.

He watched Miss Culpepper stop and laugh as she tugged on the tarp. Colin was doing all the work. Suspiciously, Sling watched Colin and realized Colin was not watching or working for Miss Culpepper. He was watching Fredricka.

Colin wouldn't allow Fredricka to touch the tarp. He sat her on top of the waist-high wooden railing around the roof, shook his finger in her sassy face and scolded her. Then he gestured. She was to watch. And he checked her constantly to be sure she didn't move. Colin was not interested in Miss Culpepper.

But he let the other three women tug on the tarp. They were ineffective. They laughed. Colin showed off his muscles and slid sly, smug glances over at his wife who looked pretty sly and smug herself.

Sling pondered. With the demonstration of neighborliness from the social powers, how was he going to keep Miss Culpepper from feeling so at home?

Several days later, Chin came home from his bout with ptomaine. He had to endure the merciless teasing of the men. He was paler, and no one encouraged him to cook.

So it wasn't until two days after that, that Sling went to the Home and drove Miss Penny over to the grandparents' house. Miss Culpepper's car was there, so Miss Culpepper should also be there.

Leaving his guest in the truck, Sling exited the pickup and went up the steps, making his boots thunder in announcing his advance. Then he boomed his steps across the porch. That was deliberate. Kids in Texas learned early to walk softly on wooden floors or their mothers got really ticked off.

On top of that, he rattled the door with his fist. Overkill.

A voice came out of the sky. "Yes?"

He had to step back, then he had to retreat to the yard to look up. There she was. Miss Culpepper. Her blond tresses teased by the flirting breeze, her scoop-neck blouse gaping.

Sling considered that if he was level with her, he would be able to see down her blouse at those rounds that hung so nicely from her chest. He stared, caught by the idea.

She watched him as she would a two-headed calf. Again she inquired, "Yes?"

He understood that she was being put-offish with him. He said, "I've brought Miss Penny to share this house and help you by chaperoning you. You are a woman alone, and Miss Penny will help you keep up appearances."

With his words, he had implied that she was a loose woman; besides being a woman who stole houses, her morals were suspect.

She said, "I beg your pardon?"

"Apology accepted."

"I was not apologizing to you for anything. I was indicating that you are on my property without my permission and that you are completely out of line."

"I'll go get the sheriff."

"Why?"

"I'm on the board at the Golden Years Home. Like you, Miss Penny is homeless. If I can suffer you here until you find another place, then you will have to share with Miss Penny."

Miss Culpepper stood straight and looked down her nose at Sling Mueller. She looked off into the distance. Then she turned her head and looked farther. Finally she looked back at the slouched, dark and dangerous figure of the tall and sinfully handsome Sling Mueller. She said, "I'll come down."

"You bet you will," he muttered, and his lips almost smiled.

Three

Miss Culpepper came out on the porch as serene as if she owned the whole damned place. She was curious about the fragile and bent Miss Penny, who did not say a word as she doggedly climbed the front steps to the porch.

With some impulsive macho moves that showed off his body, Sling took Miss Penny's luggage out of the back of the pickup and carried them up the steps. He then escorted Miss Penny into the house. He said "Pardon us" to Miss Culpepper and went past her as he indicated to Miss Penny that she was to go up the stairs to the second floor.

Miss Culpepper followed. Her curiosity was mixed with a great deal of indignation and a touch of amusement. At the top of the stairs, Sling gestured to the doors of rooms that led from the hall and asked the probably three-hundred-year-old lady, "Which room would you like?"

Miss Culpepper mentioned: "That one is mine."

Shaking his head, Sling pointed to Miss Culpepper's claimed room and relayed that information to Miss Penny. "She's claimed the master bedroom."

Miss Culpepper exclaimed, "'Master'? It's the same size as the others."

Sling ignored her. "How about this one?" he asked Miss Penny. "On the east side, this way, it's shaded from the evening sun. Is it okay?"

Miss Penny's dried bird head turned in limited jerks as she inspected the neat room, and she finally nodded.

Sling set the box and suitcase down inside the room and said, "I hope you're very happy here."

Miss Penny patted his arm. She went into the room and closed the door.

Miss Culpepper frowned. "Won't she need some help, sorting her things out and putting them away?"

Sling was quite aware that Miss Culpepper never once made any objection to having Miss Penny there. "No," Sling replied in an aloof manner. "She's not senile nor is she helpless. She's here so that you have a chaperon."

Miss Culpepper blinked and frowned incredulously. "You're not serious."

"You've had all sorts of men over here every single day. Any more of that and your reputation will be shot all to hell. Since I can't come over here to supervise you, I found Miss Penny to guard your morals."

"I don't believe this."

He lifted both hands, palms out and turned his face modestly aside. "Don't thank me. It was my duty since you are living under my jurisdiction."

Her words went awry. "Muph, gogmt." She took a steadying breath. "I won't stand for this."

"You're going to throw Miss Penny out? Go ahead. I'll get my camera. It'll look great in court. A video-tape would be better. Would you wait until I go home for the camera?"

Miss Culpepper drew in an indignant breath.

"No? Well, stills will do. I'll go on out." He started busily away but paused to ask, "Could I suggest that you wait until she's off the steps before you toss out her opened suitcase? That'd make a better visual."

"You *BEAST!*"

"I am not, either! I'm a good man who put up with your *unknown-to-you* bloodsucking relative for over twenty-five of her sixty-seven years of harassment of the fine Mueller family. I'm not going to have you setting up a house of ill-repute in the Mueller grand-parents' house, and that's final."

Miss Culpepper shrieked and clutched her fists into her hair.

With concern, Sling said, "I believe you're unsta-ble. It could be this heat. Texas is one step down into hell, they say, and if you can't stand these preliminar-ies, take warning."

"You are impossible! Will you leave?"

"I'll be waiting with my camera." He then went out to his pickup, opened both doors, put on the boom box loudly enough so that no matter where she went on that section of his property, she wouldn't be able not to hear him. And he lay across the front seat with his Stetson over his face and his booted feet on the windowsill of the open door.

His strangely marked liver-spotted dog wandered around for a while, then came back to lie in the shade under the truck.

It was evening. It was getting late, but days lingered in the summer. It was hot and muggy. It was the kind of weather that tested non-Texans.

As dusk settled, Sling went up the front steps in his boot-thundering manner and boomed across the porch before he knocked. He smiled.

Eventually, after the second knock had long since rattled away into oblivion, Miss Culpepper came to the hooked screen door. He said, "It's getting late and the light's failing. Could you do the eviction of Miss Penny tomorrow? The light would be best about ten-thirty."

"Go jump in the creek."

He smiled. "No water."

With false sweetness, she suggested: "Find a high place over a rock bottom."

"I need to reassure Miss Penny that she can sleep peacefully tonight."

Miss Culpepper hesitated. "Is she mute?" She asked that with care.

"No."

"She doesn't speak," Miss Culpepper told him.

He replied kindly. "She's that rarity in females. She doesn't speak unless she has something to say."

"Goodbye, Mr. Mueller." Miss Culpepper turned away from the still-hooked screen door. Over her shoulder, she added: "See you in court."

* * *

Miss Penny hadn't called Sling by the next morning so Sling did what he had to do about his place. But on off times, he watched through the telescope out the attic vent just to keep track.

In the next days those two illegal occupants were out and about. Miss Culpepper's little white car was always buzzing away or returning. Then he noted that She had Miss Penny in the car out on his lower meadow, and She had Miss Penny *driving* that car! What the hell was That Woman up to?

He drove the wide circle of the road over there and thundered up onto the porch to knock teeth-rattlingly, and there was no answer. Keeping to the porch, Sling walked around the whole house. The meadow was empty. Her car was gone. No one was anywhere around. In the time it had taken him to drive from his place out to the road and come around, She'd slipped off somewhere.

He thudded his boots down off the porch, got into his pickup and drove off. He was so restless and irritated that he went out along the fence line where a couple of his men were burning thornbushes. He nodded but was silent. He helped for a while with the burning of the weeds. Then he gathered a bunch of those scorched but still-recognizable devil's thorns and put them in his truck.

He lifted a hand in farewell to the silent, intensely curious men, then he got into the pickup and drove up to the county cemetery. He spread the sterile thorn branches on Lizzie's grave and said in an irritated voice, "You really have the last laugh, don't you, you old biddy?"

On his way back home, he stopped off at the Mueller family plot on a part of their land. It was an old, old gathering of Muellers over almost four hundred years. The variety of headstones and names was a wonder.

He went to his parents' graves as he'd done in times of stress in these past fifteen years, and he told them all about Miss Culpepper and warned his dad not to laugh because he was in no mood to allow that. Before he left, he said he wished they were back with him; he had a problem.

Sling was a disgruntled man. He went to bed at night restless and irritated, but a soothing sound was carried on the gentle Gulf breeze that spoke of adventure and love and magic. Songs of the mermaids? The lure of the sea in that dry land? He immersed himself in the sound and settled down. In his sleep, he smiled.

During each day, Sling spent some time in the attic, watching that Woman's doings. There was never a letup of traffic at the grandparents' house. That next day, Colin and Fredricka were there for twenty minutes at least. Ethel and Natalie were there the day after that, and Ned came the following morning. The Mueller hand, *Tom,* was there briefly that afternoon! She obviously had hordes of visitors, as anyone could plainly see.

Who had been there with her when he hadn't been watching?

How had Miss Culpepper made such a wide and sympathetic acquaintance in so short a time? That was suspicious. Where did all those people come from? He'd surely like to know that little fact.

Whatever she was up to, he ought to interfere. So he turned the telescope away from the opened gap in the attic wall, went downstairs, out to his pickup and thought he'd just go over there and see.

But he paused at his truck. It was new and shiny and important looking. She'd think he could afford to give up that land to her without a fight. He'd take his old truck. He went into the barn and looked fondly at the vintage pickup. But it did look ratty. No woman would take a man seriously who drove a tacky truck like that one.

Then his horse came into the barn to see what Sling was doing in there.

Of course! He'd ride Tucker. Miss Culpepper was unarguably a city woman. Just look at her. She was down there in the wide-open spaces of the wild West. He'd give her a taste of it.

He lifted his Stetson and resettled it. He knew he looked good on Tucker. Tucker was smart. He looked like a Marlboro horse and nothing rattled him, not since he'd been gelded.

Tucker had been neglected in favor of the spiffy new pickup, and he was some surprised to be saddled. He bent his neck around and watched that with reservations. He didn't mind the saddle, but saddles generally meant someone was going to climb aboard and make him walk somewhere.

So when Sling led Tucker out of the barn and got on, Tucker did object a little. He threw Sling. And Spots sat watching and laughed silently.

Sling was really irritated. He sat there on the ground and said some rather colorful things to his attentive horse. Then Sling got up and walked over to Tucker and said quietly, "Don't you do that again. Do you hear me?" And his voice was serious.

Tucker danced a step or two, but Sling got on in a no-more-nonsense way, and Tucker settled down to enjoy the outing.

To just ride over the roll of land to the other house was much quicker, and her car was still on the lane. She hadn't gotten away. As they approached the crest of the dividing roll of land, Sling said to Tucker, "If you got anything to get rid of, do it now. I would be embarrassed if you should litter Miss Culpepper's—a *Mueller* yard."

But Tucker was stretching his neck so that he could see over the rim of the rise. The horse hadn't been over that way in a while and he was interested. They went down the slope and were almost to the very house when he saw the sign. It was big and it read: Mending.

Sling was taken aback. She had no income? She would have to take in mending to eat? How was he going to evict a woman who had no place to go? She could sell that sassy car and he could give her his old pickup.

He stepped down off the horse saying, "Behave, hear me?"

Tucker swished his tail and moved his back feet a little as if to show he could do as he chose. Then he bent his head and pushed at Sling in a friendly way. Sling wasn't stupid; he gave Tucker a sugar cube.

She came around the house on the porch and stood quietly, watching Sling. He became intensely aware that she was a young, good-looking, vibrant female, and that he was a male of the same species. It was unsettling. How could Lizzie have a relative that looked the way Miss Culpepper looked? Automatically, as he'd had drilled into him from birth, he briefly lifted his Stetson to Miss Culpepper; but he didn't actually take the hat off, since they were still outside.

She said, "Now what?"

He was still taken with the fact that they were of two genders. "Where're you from?"

"Bloomington, Indiana."

"Is that so. Are you a ... Yankee?"

"Born and bred." She was neutral, watching him.

He considered that was discouraging. "What'd you do, up yonder?"

"I was an instructor at Indiana University."

He considered that she could pass for a Texan, she spoke so sparse. "In what?"

"The school of music. It's the best school of music in the country."

"I *had* heard tell of that." He looked thoughtful. "In what?" He asked that cautiously.

"I assume you want to know what instrument? The flute."

"Oh." That silenced him entirely.

He was bemused that she played the flute. The area was music crazy and every time the people got together, no matter what the excuse, they took their instruments along and they managed to play.

They'd been looking for a flutist.

Did they know about her, this Miss Culpepper, who had *taught* the flute? If they did, he would *never* get rid of the woman. The whole area would land on poor Sling Mueller and make him give that woman this place just so that they could have a damned flute player. He was doomed.

He looked at her, defenseless, vulnerable.

She noted the change in him. He boggled her. "Won't you sit down?"

He saw that she had placed a reed rug on the rough porch floor and there were two rocking chairs facing outward, toward the road. He said, "Don't mind if I do." But he touched the back of the first chair until she was seated, then he, too, sat down. "This is nice."

"Thank you. It's a very nice house."

He cast a stern look in her direction. The house was a forbidden subject since it was a bone of contention between them. "It's a pile of rotten, dried-out boards."

"I love the porches."

"Why?" He squinted at her.

"To see out." She gestured. Then she added: "And the shade during the day. With the porches as they are, and as the sun moves, you can move around the house to follow the shade. It's very pleasant. And to go up on the roof in the evening is lovely."

"Up there?" He frowned a little. "Why?"

"You can see farther. The breeze catches you freely."

That made him look at what the breeze would touch on her. Then he looked out to the safety of the empty road. "This is a lonesome place for two women."

"I feel such compassion for Cousin Eileen."

There she was again, bringing up touchy subjects! "You mean Lizzie?"

"Yes. Do you know why she was called Lizzie?" Miss Culpepper inquired.

"She'd been known by that name ever since she moved in on the Muellers, long long ago."

"How did that happen?"

"I surely to goodness don't know. She was a parasite."

"But your family allowed her to stay here," Miss Culpepper mentioned. "Why did you?"

"She was just another problem I inherited."

"Did she drive a car?"

"Not that I know about."

Miss Culpepper was silent.

Sling wondered if anyone had ever tried to teach Lizzie to drive. She had been trapped there in that isolated house, dependent on someone else for everything she'd needed—

Miss Culpepper inquired kindly, "Where did you go to college? Texas, probably. A. and M.?" It would be one or the other.

"No."

"You didn't go to college?"

"No."

"I've heard how you put all your brothers and sisters through school."

"Yes." His voice was stubborn with pride in that accomplishment.

"But you're the eldest. Why didn't you?"

"It was a troubled time for us. I was head of the house, and I couldn't leave the kids here without somebody to take care of them. I was the one responsible. I had to see to them. What they ate, who they saw, who their friends were. That they did their chores and learned what they needed to know. I read their books to be sure they were learning right."

"Ahhh."

"How come you're taking in mending?" He indicated the big sign.

"Not I. Miss Penny feels idle and would like something to do."

"Everybody will think it's you, and the men will be ripping seams on new shirts and pulling off buttons."

"Miss Penny will be pleased. She's a nice woman. Thank you for bringing her here."

That jarred Sling. "You two getting along okay?"

"I'm teaching her to drive."

"Good gravy! That old lady?"

"She can see with her new glasses."

"She couldn't see?" He was shocked he hadn't known that.

"Not at a distance. But now she can. And she loves driving. It frees her."

Sling didn't say anything for a time. Then he said, "That was nice of you."

"She's stone-deaf."

"I had no idea. She replied to me."

"What?"

"She said, 'Thank you.'"

"From what I've heard, you've been taking care of a lot of people for a long time."

"It wasn't a chore."

"I meant those besides your own family."

"There was nobody else to do it." He shrugged that off and went on. "Most of my sisters and brothers are married and have families or are starting them."

"Not you?"

He took his hat almost off and resettled it as men did who were a little uncomfortable. "I've been doing something like that for a long time with my sisters and brothers. Now, I'm free."

She nodded. "I can understand."

"You been taking care of family?"

"An aunt." She looked over at him.

"She die?"

Miss Culpepper smiled. "No. She got new hips and knees put in and she's off to Hawaii." She laughed in her delight at that. "She'll probably learn to hula."

"No kidding?"

Miss Culpepper agreed. "No kidding."

"I think you may be a miracle worker." He studied her for a minute and then he said firmly, "But this land is mine."

"We'll see." She dismissed the contention. "It must have been very hard for you to raise all those kids when there was no one on whom you could depend to help out."

"It's been interesting."

"There were no problems? Just work?"

"If you've been around students all this time, then you know there's always problems. The lure of playing hooky from chores or studying. Their involvements with guys that are no good for them."

"My aunt behaved herself." Miss Culpepper was droll.

"Our worst one was Kit, who got Jenny pregnant and married her. I had to be...aloof, so as she wouldn't hang on my arm when he was away at school. The others, being around, helped in that. Jenny tends to turn to the strongest man nearby. It's just her way. Kit got her figured by hisself and he sees to it that he's the man who solves things for her."

"And it works." Miss Culpepper watched Sling Mueller.

"She cottons to him."

"Cottons?"

"Ever pick cotton?"

"No."

"It sticks all over you." He sighed. "I just shudder at all you've got to learn and ... How old are you?"

"Twenty-nine."

"You're getting a late start in learning about living by yourself." He shook his head sadly. "Guess I'll have to sign you on to pick some cotton so as you can begin to learn how things relate in our language."

She gave him a patient look. "And I'll teach you to sew."

"I thought Miss Penny was going to do the mending."

"She does the things that need the sewing machine. I was speaking of needlework so that you can begin to learn all the things you don't know."

He ignored Miss Culpepper's sassiness. "You got her a sewing machine?"

"With mending, especially men's things, the mender needs the closer, stronger stitching of a machine."

"You've been very kind to that old lady."

"You gave me no choice."

He narrowed his eyes. "Are you trying to make me squirm?"

"Never." She even smiled at him.

He guessed: "You think I'll get that done all by myself."

She tried not to widen her small smile and had to bite her lower lip.

He watched that. Then he surprised himself by asking, "You got any extra water? I'm a little thirsty."

"Would you like some lemonade?"

"No beer?"

"I can't corrupt Miss Penny."

With that rather snippy response, Miss Culpepper went into the the house, and Sling found himself wondering what her first name night be. How could she be living in his house with him not knowing her first name? He couldn't just out-and-out ask her. It would make him appear interested in her. And he wasn't.

He sat there in the silence, watching his horse wander around, with Spots keeping tabs on the larger animal.

Nobody went by on the road. It was peaceful.

The birds were around. A scissortail was on the single telephone wire that ended at her hou—that ended there. This was a lonesome place. There wasn't a barn or a shed. Just the house, sitting out in the middle of a treeless space. Treeless, because that Lizzie had cut down those fine oaks without a word to him. That fact still rankled.

Miss Culpepper came out onto the porch carrying a tray with two glasses. Sling got up and went to help her. He took the tray until she sat down, then he gave her a glass, took the other and leaned the tray against the porch rail.

It was a fine porch rail. It was just the right height for a contented man in a rocking chair to lean back and prop his feet up on it. Sling cast a quick glance over at Miss Culpepper.

Did she know that the winds pressed her dress against her that way? Is that why she always wore dresses? She knew that the soft material showed off her figure, making a man's glances move over her? And the taunting breeze played with her flirty skirts, which shifted and flipped and billowed naughtily, making a man think about those skirts lifting?

He glanced up her body to her face and she was watching him with a level look. He blushed. He thought maybe Miss Culpepper might not be a flirt. She looked exactly like a schoolteacher with a student who wasn't very mature. He reminded himself that he was some years older, and she ought not to be so sure he was looking at her in that particular way.

He looked out along the empty road. "You get much traffic past here?" He made conversation.

"No. Only some visitors."

Yeah. All those men trooping in to look at how the wind taunted them by moving her soft dress.

He finished the last of the lemonade and stood up. She didn't move. He said, "Thank you for the lemonade."

"You're welcome."

He again almost lifted his Stetson as he handed her his empty glass. "I'll be getting along."

"Goodbye."

She didn't invite him to stay or suggest he have dinner or anything. She just nodded in agreement that he was leaving.

He went over to the steps and whistled for Tucker. Did the horse hustle up and come on over? No. He glanced over his shoulder as if inquiring why his master had whistled.

Sling slouched and said with great forbearance, "The danged horse hasn't been ridden enough and he thinks he's a liberated horse."

She only looked over to where the horse was still waiting for a confirmation of the command.

Sling set his hat more firmly and wondered if the damned horse was going to try to throw him again. With his hands on his hips in an inordinately serious stance, Sling whistled again, softly.

Softer was more serious.

The horse trotted over, his ears forward. Curious.

Sling never gave the horse a chance. He treated Tucker as if he'd just been introduced to the saddle and a rider. Sling mounted, no-nonsense, and sat down, ready. The horse behaved as if they were old friends who could be casual with each other.

As he nudged Tucker's sides gently, Sling touched his hat to Miss Culpepper.

But she was bent over, retrieving the tray, and hadn't noticed Sling's great control of an animal that outweighed him about five or six times.

So all the way home over the roll of land, Sling listed Tucker's faults to him. The horse trotted along, looking around, twitching his ears to catch the more colorful phrases. And Spots kept up, running alongside, being the staunch and loyal friend.

Sling got back to the house to rampant chaos.

As soon as Sling saw the men running in and out of the house, he ran Tucker flat out. Fire?

Sling arrived in the yard by jumping Tucker over a fence and skittering him to a rather impressive halt.

Too bad she couldn't have seen that! But he ran up onto the porch and hollered, "What?"

A distracted hand yelled, "Somehow the vent fell out of the attic opening, and there are about fifty dozen birds in the house!"

Four

Actually, there were only five or six birds inside. It only seemed as if there were more because the birds had panicked, flying into windows and mirrors.

Sling shouted to the men: "Stop!"

They froze.

"Settle down," Sling said softly. "You know better than this. Shoo them individually."

Chin, a Chinese who was a fifth-generation American, stood with his hands in his sleeves and his eyes narrowed as he intoned, "Birds in house are good omen."

Tom retorted, "Birds in house, poop."

Sling calmed them. "Just be gentle."

It took a while. Each room had to have a window screen removed and that had to be done from outside. The men groused and did it. As a bird got into a room, the door was closed, the shades were pulled down on all the other windows and the bird was coaxed out the open window.

And the entire time, Sling was inventing and discarding reasons for the attic vent having been unprotected and why the telescope was there beside the opening. It was so betraying. What else was there to look out of that opening but Miss Culpepper?

When Sling finally went up to the attic, he was followed by several of the men. Sling had told the men, "Never mind. I can handle it."

But they had replied, "There might be a couple more of them still up there."

There weren't any birds, only Chin. Chin smiled his enigmatic grimace and said, "The slatted barrier slipped out."

It was back in place. The first quick glance around had shown Sling that the telescope was now on the other side of the attic where it had always been. He gave Chin a studying look but said nothing.

But as Chin passed Sling, going down the steps, Sling growled at him. "If you dare to grow a droopy Charlie Chan mustache, the boys and I will shave it off—on one side."

Chin said, "Velly good."

Sling replied, "Watch it."

Since one of the rules of the household was to check in and check out, *without fail,* Sling then said, "I have to see Colin Kilgallon."

Not waiting for any remark that Chin might have, Sling went out to unsaddle his horse and found that had been done. Tucker came over and demanded a sugar cube. Sling gave it to him, knowing full well that whoever had unsaddled the horse had already given him the prerequisite cube.

Sling got into his shiny new pickup and drove down the dusty road toward the Kilgallons' house. As he drove along, he considered the people who lived on his place. He knew of households that were normal. Why was his made up of such a weird bunch of individuals? There were people who had perfectly ordinary horses. But look at his horse. How did anybody begin to explain why Sling Mueller had been saddled with the people and animals on his place who were such eccentrics?

Sling mulled that over for several miles and decided to have their water tested.

Fredricka greeted Sling with "Pigeon pie tonight?"

Sling stared, mentally flipping through the men at his place, wondering who had called ahead. "Not tonight."

Fredricka asked: "Coffee?"

"Please," Sling replied.

"Ragtail came by with a whole slew of pigeons." Fredricka explained. "He's culling his flock. You're welcome to stay."

See? Guilty conscience influenced perception. He altered his thinking. "I just might."

Fredricka handed Sling two big full cups of coffee. "Colin's down by the barn. Know anything about transmissions?"

"Everything." He'd kept cars and trucks running all during the lean years.

"Good. He can use you."

So it turned into a pleasant afternoon. Both men were in and out from under the truck getting very dirty, talking about everything in the world and even occasionally discussing transmissions.

After a time, though, Colin mentioned: "Saw your horse over at Miss Culpepper's. You sparking that gal?"

In the whole time Sling had been at her house, not one car had passed by there. How had Colin known he'd been there on Tucker? He said very casually, "Just neighborly."

"That's some woman," Colin commented. "Umm-umph!"

"Does Fredricka know about this?"

"Fredricka knows all about Clovis."

"Clovis?"

"Miss Culpepper."

Clovis. Her name was Clovis. Spicy. It was just right. Then Sling asked suspiciously, "Why does Fredricka 'know all about'... Clovis?"

Colin was astonished. "She's a flutist."

They knew.

The shock of that went through Sling. He'd never get rid of her, not now. And Sling felt light-headed. "You know?"

"Now you *have* to know we've been beating the bushes for a flutist?"

Sling felt compelled to say, "You've gotten along all right up until now."

"Oboes and flutes go together."

Sling asked sourly, "And Fred knows about all this oboe-and-flute business?"

"Fredricka likes Clovis."

"Fred was always a little dense."

Colin cautioned softly, "Now, Sling..."

"How'd you know about Clovis playing the flute?"

Colin turned his greasy face toward Sling and even stopped the wrench. "Didn't you see it the first day? It was in its case on the passenger side of the front seat...with the seat belt around it. That showed how much she loves that flute. You *had* to've seen that! Why else would we have helped her move into her house?"

"The Mueller house."

"She has papers," Colin warned.

"Fraudulent."

"If you can prove that, we'll find her another place. You ought to hear her play. It pulls up memories from back when we all lived in the sea."

Wonder stirred in Sling. He'd been going to sleep at night with lost memories of the sea. Had it been *her* flute coming from across the way? Had... Clovis... been sitting on her rooftop like an ages-past lure to the sea? And Colin had heard it, too? "When did you hear her play?" He heard jealousy in his voice. Distracted by that, he almost didn't hear Colin's reply.

"Right away. We teased her for fastening it down with the belt thataway. And she got it out and played for us. It was after you left. You should have hung around. She gave us each a beer."

Clovis had told him she didn't have beer around to corrupt Miss Penny, but she'd given the others a beer. So Sling's voice was sour as he said, "How nice."

"Now, now. Don't you go casting aspersions on that lady."

When Colin used that soft tone, it was dangerous. Sling asked with equal softness, "You set yourself up as her protector?"

"No." Colin's voice was still gentle. "But Fredricka did. She and her mother, Ethel, and Ethel's bosom friend, Natalie. What more protection could a single lady want?"

That was a challenge. "A man's." Sling gave Colin a rather hostile look.

"There'll be more than aplenty of those around. Watch."

"Yeah?" Sling became silent. He didn't leave or quit helping, but he became thoughtful, sorting things out in his mind.

So at supper, as they shared the pigeon pies and he waited for the opportunity to speak about Clovis, he was still rather sparse in his responses.

Finally Fredricka said, "I've asked Clovis to join us at the square dance next weekend. She doesn't know anyone around here, and that'll be a good place for her to start becoming acquainted."

And Sling's words trod right in on the end of Fredricka's sentence. "I'll take her."

"Oh," said Fredricka.

Colin soothed Sling, telling him: "Don't fret yourself. It would be awkward for you to do that when you're trying to evict her."

"If I don't take her to the dance, some yahoo will."

"Tim knows better. He's said so."

"There are other yahoos around here besides Tim."

"Oh?" Colin was fascinated by the idea. "Who? I thought we had a pretty good bunch of people around here."

"They are. But Clovis shouldn't have any dealings with the riffraff. She can do better than that."

"Who?"

"How the hell should I know?" Sling's temper was rising.

Colin put his hands up and raised his eyebrows. "I was just taking suggestions to get her together with someone suitable."

"Matchmaking!" Sling accused.

"Now, what's wrong with that?"

The two Kilgallons were fascinated. Who had ever before seen Sling angry? Old, easygoing, nothing-bothered-him Sling Mueller was a little red-faced and breathing in an upset manner. Great. The husband and wife exchanged a quick glance and an almost-smile.

Sling saw that and was briefly silent. He had no idea why he was reacting so strongly to the idea of another man escorting...Clovis to the square dance. He sorted it out and steadied down.

With calm logic, he said, "You have to know she has a claim on a portion of my land. You also know there was no way we could get rid of Lizzie until she died. It took three generations to wait her out. Now her cousin is here, claiming the land. If some free-loader squires Clovis around and marries her, we could have a whole new problem. We Muellers might never get rid of them. They'd proliferate like rabbits and outlast us. It's better that I keep a firm hand on the woman until this is settled."

Calmly, Sling looked up at the attentive couple. They were mesmerized. They smiled and said variations of "Right" and "Good idea." They even acted as if they had been a part of the decision.

Sling eyed the pair and thought maybe his household wasn't the only bunch of weirdos around.

He went back to his place after supper, and all was calm. That was a relief. Tucker and Spots came out and greeted him as he put the pickup away in the barn. He petted them both, and they followed Sling to the gate. The dog came through it, but the horse was willing to stay in the barnyard . . . fortunately.

Spots didn't go into the house. He was strictly a yard dog. Sling left him on the porch and went into the silent house. It was peaceful. He moved tired shoulders as he walked through to his room and turned on a light.

There, blinking and shifting its feet, a bird was roosting on the headboard of his bed.

Under his breath, Sling said a word that his mother had always forbidden, but he said it in a soothing way, turned off the light and closed the door. How could he run that day bird out into the night? It would be disoriented. It was settled there. He'd leave it.

On the off chance the bird would waken before he did in the morning, Sling repeated the tactics they had used earlier. Without a light, he quietly, quietly went outside to remove the screen, then returned and opened the window. Then he got ready for bed in the dark, crawled into his bed, with his head at the other end, whispering a warning to the bird not to dirty up his blanket, and he went to sleep.

And Sling dreamed struggles. Into his sleeping mind came all sorts of vague challenges that he fought and strove against. Nothing was clear as to why he was having such a bad time, and he wakened exhausted.

The bird was gone.

He put the screen back and was aware that the only good thing about the dry, parched weather was that there were no mosquitoes. With that lesser food source, plus the scant supply of weeds, there were also fewer birds. Each one left was valuable.

As he showered and dressed, he hesitated, took down a beloved old soft shirt and calmly ripped the shoulder seam. Then he took off two buttons. He smiled as if he were clever. Clovis would never guess he'd been deliberate—not after he had said men would do just that sort of thing as an excuse to go to her place.

Right after breakfast, he clarified what his people had scheduled for the day. Then he went "to town"— he said—but he drove over to Clovis's...to where she was staying.

As he came to the road and turned onto it, he realized almost immediately that it was far too early to visit anyone, much less go into town. That made him uncomfortable. Well, he'd get gas. They had a pump on the Home Place, but it wouldn't hurt to see Bud at his station and catch up on the gossip. First he'd just drive by the place. He'd see if she was up. Then he could drive by again after he got the gas. Would she notice?

As his pickup approached the house, he could see that she was up on the roof and looking his way. He could see her.

He slowed. Then he relaxed, driving rather negligently as he eased his truck along the road. He turned into the lane, keeping track of her out of the corner of his eye. She saw him, all right.

He rolled the pickup to a quiet stop, and he was slow in exiting the truck. But he did get out and stretch, moving his shoulders as if he'd been working for hours by then. He glanced up, and there she was, watching him.

He walked over until he stood just below her. He put his hat on the back of his head and his hands on his hips. His tongue said, "Rapunzel, Rapunzel, let down your hair."

She leaned her elbows on the railing, the neck of her dress gaping down so wastefully at that height.

He asked softly, "What are you doing up there?"

"Looking at the countryside." She spoke in a natural way.

With her words, Sling understood Miss Penny couldn't hear them and they needn't be quiet.

His clever tongue said, "I thought you might need help."

"No. If I did, I'd hang out my red petticoat."

"That would get attention." He walked a pace or two, then he asked, "Want to ride with me to the gas station?" And as soon as the words were out, he blushed. That was so high school that he couldn't believe his clever tongue was that stupid. He lowered his head so that his Stetson would block her view of that betraying flush.

"That would be exciting." She was kind. "It's too early to go running around the countryside with a strange man."

"I'm ordinary." He looked up into her face. His quickly soothing words were solemn.

She laughed softly in the most disturbingly thrilling sound his senses had ever heard.

"I've never ravished an unwilling woman."

"Ahhh." She made that nothing word sound full of understanding and undercurrents of knowledge.

"Somebody been talking to you about me?"

She tilted her head as she appeared to consider, to search her memory. Then she said, "No. Am I missing gossip?"

"No, ma'am. I'm an upstanding citizen. You'd be safe with me."

She only smiled.

Then he realized that she was still up there, and he was still standing on the ground below. She hadn't said anything about coming down or him going up there to her.

She was keeping her distance. She was leery of him?

He said to her in a reassuring manner, "We're on a semisabbatical over at my place. If you have anything heavy to move or something stymies you, call and we'll find someone to come over here and help you." Him.

"No problems." She said that firmly. Then she inquired hesitantly: "A semi...sabbatical?"

"To give the land and the men a rest. You know how dry it's been. We sold off most of the herds, and we're letting everything just...rest. We only do maintenance."

"That's unusual."

"The land needs it. We've had good years, and a lot of hard work. We're all taking turns going out and away to do something different."

"Where are you going?"

"Only here. I don't need a rest from it. I love this land." He looked up at her. "All of it." He was serious.

She smiled just a bit. "Got it."

He wondered if she meant that she understood his emphasis on all of his land, or if she was saying that she wasn't giving up her claim. Well. He'd made himself clear. He'd wait and see what she did next. He inquired, "Need anything from town?"

"No. Thank you. We're going in later."

"Be glad to save you the trip." .

"No. Miss Penny loves shopping. She needs some thread for her mending."

"Oh." He was suddenly reminded and made it sound that way. "I have a shirt for her."

"She'll be pleased. Put it on the rocker on the porch."

"You're not coming down?" He was a little embarrassed to urge her that way.

"This is the time to mend my soul."

His voice was gentle. "Whatever have you been doing that it needs mending? Are you serious?"

"Not really. My life has been very hectic and this peace is soaking into me."

He thought how he'd like to "soak" into her. He *would!* And he looked up at her in a different way.

Her head was turned, as she looked off to the side away from him. But she didn't leave the railing. She didn't just walk off out of his sight.

But she didn't come down, either.

"Well, if you're sure you don't need anything?"

"Thanks, anyway."

"No trouble." He resettled his Stetson and went back to his truck, got into it and drove away, aware of how disappointed he was.

That sobered him. He not only wanted her body, he wanted her? No. It was just that she was a challenge. He'd get her, sleep with her, oust her from his property and give her a goodbye gift as he let her go. That was what a man did.

What would he get for her? What would he give Miss Culpepper as a farewell gift? And he saw her naked on his bed as he draped her body in pearls.

He almost ran into the ditch.

Then, when he got home, he noticed he hadn't left the shirt for Miss Penny, after all. He'd have to go back.

He smiled.

With stern self-discipline, Sling didn't go over the hill to see Miss Culpepper again for two whole, restless, irritating days. Especially frustrating was the fact that he couldn't bring himself to go up into his own attic and remove his own slatted vent and put his own telescope to the opening so that he could watch her in his own house. He grumped around.

Chin asked, "You need physic?"

And Sling thundered: *"No!"*

"You act so."

Sling snapped, "You can talk English."

"Ah, so."

"What'd you say?" The words were snarled.

Chin smiled as he spelled it out: *"A-h, s-o."*

Sling put his finger on Chin's chest and tapped it with each threatening word. "You really walk the edge around here. You'd better watch your step."

For some reason, that sent Chin into a fit of laughter.

Sling knew he had to get the water tested.

It was Saturday, a week before the square dance, when Sling finally took his shirt back over to be mended. He had added a pair of jeans that were disreputable. Clean but tacky.

When he got out of his truck, he saw that a used shed had been added to the side yard. If he had just looked out the attic opening, he would have noticed that. The shed had been brought there from some place else. Why hadn't Clovis asked for help?

Sling walked over to it and eyed the weathered shed. No puny women had wrestled that shed into place. It had taken a truck to carry it. Some men had delivered it there. Who? Sling went back to go up onto the porch, carrying the shirt and jeans in one clenched hand, and he pounded on the door with the other clenched hand.

Miss Penny came to the door and smiled as she held it open for him to enter. He did that.

He looked around and listened, but he could hear no sound. Her car was out back. Sling looked at Miss Penny, who was standing down there with her face turned up to his, watching him.

He showed her the places that needed mending on his shirt and jeans. She took them in her bird-claw hands and nodded, still smiling. Then she said in her cracked voice, "Clovis is out yonder." And she gestured.

Sling didn't hug the old lady, but he beamed down on her. With restraint, he just nodded once and walked on out the back door. Just outside, there She was, wearing shorts and a loose shirt. She was opening a can of paint.

He went over to her and put his hands on his hips. "What do you think you're doing?"

She looked around to him and said, "Well, hello." And she smiled.

He forgot what he'd been about to say.

She gestured with her brush. "We have a new shed. I'm going to paint it purple."

His face muscles flinched involuntarily.

She laughed up at him in pure delight. "That's what the others did. Why is purple wrong for a chicken shed?"

"Chic-kens?" He was appalled.

She said musingly, "They said that, too, just that way."

"I'm not surprised."

"It'll be beautiful," she assured him.

"Did you get permission from the owner to do this?"

"No. He would flinch. And then he'd argue. And finally he would refuse."

"So you agree that I own this place."

"Not at all. We are alone and you can't prove that I said anything. You aren't wired. You would have no proof at all."

"You're a sneaky woman."

She smiled at him. "Miss Penny misses the sounds of chickens—"

"She's deaf."

"She can see. A few chickens aren't going to upset you that much, are they? We'll share the eggs."

"Eggs?" He was stunned. "Haven't you ever heard of coyotes? This is a land of heat, sticker burrs, snakes of all kinds, *and coyotes!* How long do you think chickens will last here? You'll be wiped out in a week."

"Could I borrow your dog until I get the fence up?"

"FENCE!"

"That wasn't something to mention." She guessed that right away. "I've always heard that cattlemen don't care for fences. I thought it was an exaggeration. Apparently it isn't."

"You may not build a fence on my land."

"How am I going to keep the chickens from straying?"

"By not getting any chickens." He made his measured voice calm and logical.

"But they *are* ordered, and I *have* paid for them."

He did some ordering of his own: "Send them back."

"They are already on their way here. I can't return them. Will the coyotes really eat them?"

His voice was steady. "Either the coyotes or the snakes."

"I just wanted Miss Penny to enjoy living here with me. She was raised on a farm. She remembers the chickens, the roosters crowing and her being allowed to gather the eggs in a basket."

"That was no call for you to buy chickens."

"You're the one who brought Miss Penny to me. I assumed you wanted me to treat her well."

"Chickens were not a part of the deal."

"We didn't have any 'deal', if you will recall that. You just dropped her off here."

"Did they run you out of Indiana?"

She licked her lips and looked around as she tried to come up with a really stunning setdown for him, but she couldn't think of a thing, so she said, "Yes."

"I'm not surprised. And I'll bet it was the women who carried the pitchforks, nudging you along."

"Yes." She pretended to look off, away from him, but she knew she had his attention, and she flicked her eyebrows a bit and pushed out her lower lip. She added: "They objected to my red satin petticoat."

"It was what was under that petticoat they objected to. How many men have you ruined?"

"I'm working on my first one." She lifted her chin and gave him a very saucy look.

Right then, he could have kissed her until she went completely wild. She was just lucky he had control. He said in a threat, "No chickens."

"You're too late." She looked at her watch. "They'll be here in about an hour."

He hadn't raised all his brothers and sisters and not learned anything. He told her, "Go ahead and paint the shed. The smell will give them the pip."

She went blank. Then she frowned. "Really?" she asked suspiciously.

"Go ahead. Paint it." He looked at his watch. "You just have enough time to slap a coat on the outside."

"How can I be sure you're telling the truth?"

"Too bad it's Saturday. You could call the Farm Bureau and check me out."

"What's a farm bureau?"

He resettled his hat in perfectly mimed disgust. "And you want to raise chickens."

"Well, what should I do?"

"You can't send them back?"

"No. I really can't." She looked at him fully, her brown eyes candid.

"Then you can put them in the shed and close the door and tomorrow invite all your acquaintances over for chicken dinner."

"You are heartless."

He shook his head. "I've never met these chickens. I could eat one without a qualm."

"You're assuming I would invite you?"

"Tenants always invite the landlord over to a meal."

"I'm not paying you rent."

He looked at her and tucked his lower lip under his upper teeth. "We might work a deal."

Five

___

Sling stood there and waited. He'd just given Clovis an opening to reply all sorts of suggestions. Instead, she picked up the can of paint and walked slowly over to the tacky shed. She was going to paint it ... purple.

His whole backbone and nervous system flinched. Purple. He tried to think of some tactful way to prevent her from doing that in order to delay until he could get a better argument going.

She bent over to put the can on a board, and Sling lost track of his plotting.

She'd put five swipes on the roof of the shed before Sling realized she wasn't using paint; it was preservative. Preservative? On that porous, rotten assortment of boards? He said, "I thought you said purple."

"Disappointed?"

"Relieved."

"This is just the base coat." She went on painting.

"You don't always tell the truth."

"I lied about being run out of Indiana, and you didn't suspect that."

He resettled his Stetson, put his hands on the backs of his hips and scanned the horizon. "Any woman that looks like you do would garner the irritation of any sour woman."

She paused in her painting and turned her shoulders so that she could turn her head enough to look up at him. "Why, Mr. Mueller! I do believe you have handed me a most gracious compliment." Her fake Southern drawl rather spoiled her honeyed response.

Sling accepted it. "What else have you lied about?"

"I'm twenty-six."

"Oh?" Sling frowned at her.

"I went to the Farm Bureau last week and researched chickens. I haven't yet ordered them." She looked up at him. "I know what causes pip in chickens."

"Uh—"

"I am a flutist. I inherited this property."

He examined the horizon again. "I can tell right now that you're going to be a trial."

"Get a good lawyer."

He frowned at her quickness. "Now, that *is* something you ought to think about," he told her. "With the scam you're running on me, you're going to need a genius. I'd suggest that you get—"

"I've already retained an attorney. Greg Thompson has agreed to defend my claim."

"What? Greg's *my* lawyer!"

"Not in this case."

Sling took off his hat and threw it on the ground. "I'll be damned."

"More than likely." Her voice was complacent.

"We'll just see about this." He scooped up his hat, banged it against his knee to dust it off and set it on his head. But before he could get out of earshot, he heard her mild, smug word: "Yes."

Greg was astonished that Sling took his representing Miss Culpepper so personal. "A buck's a buck. Your side'll be boring. This will take craftiness and guile. It'll stimulate me."

"Just see to it that it isn't Miss Culpepper that's doing the stimulating."

"Oh?" Greg grinned. "Staking a claim?"

"Not at all. I want to run her out of town." Her and her red petticoat. "If you get personal, this case could drag on forever, and she'd finally get the land on squatter's rights."

"That is a facet already."

"What?"

"Lizzie lived there for sixty-seven years."

Sling huffed. "We couldn't get rid of her!"

"We all know that, but you didn't evict her."

Sling opened out his arms. "Now, how was we supposed to do that?"

"I know. Only real cruel people can do something that mean. Oh, and Sling, you ought to know ahead of time so you're braced. We're considering trespassing and malicious-mischief charges because you invaded her property and just about ruined the plumbing when you tried to pull down Miss Culpepper's house. Do you know what it cost her to get Sweetie to come clear out there to fix it? Shocking."

Sling stared.

Greg said cheerily, "Close your mouth, you'll catch flies. You know, I always thought that meant fly balls?"

Sling though maybe it was the whole area that was off kilter. It could be the radioactive clouds from the early atomic testing out west of there. "Now, just tell me this, Greg. Who am I supposed to find to represent me?"

"My partner?"

"George? He's more argumentative than you. If I had him, you two would debate the various points and possibilities, and we'd never get this thing settled."

"She has papers, old friend."

"You have no loyalty."

"Wait, Sling. Are you taking this personal? After all we've been through?"

"Do you know how long our family has held that land?"

"It's just one little bitty corner," Greg coaxed.

"It's the principle of the thing. I'm very disappointed in you."

"Uh-oh."

"Goodbye, Greg."

And Greg said, "Keep your hands off Miss Culpepper."

Sling looked back at Greg with his jaw clenched and his eyes squinted. He didn't say anything. Then he went out the door.

In about two minutes, Greg's partner came in and leaned on the doorjamb. "I warned you. I think you just made a mistake that will haunt you the rest of your days."

"It came to whether I wanted a chance with Clovis or a friendship with Sling. In business and politics, that is always a factor. And all the years of the Mueller business and friendship went right down the drain. I want her."

"It's a betrayal of a friend. That will count against you in her evaluation. She isn't an airhead. She may look like a confection, but she's an intelligent woman. You would be wise to reconsider."

"I can't get her out of my head. I want her. I want to impress her. I want her grateful to me."

"She hasn't a prayer in this case."

"You haven't read the papers."

"I know the family. I know the circumstances. I'll offer myself to Sling to represent him."

"I'll stop it on legal ethics."

"I've already drawn up the papers to split the partnership. Like Sling, I'm disappointed in you."

Greg smiled. "It'll be an interesting fight, old buddy. And maybe I should mention that the Mueller star is fading. The burden on that land has been very heavy. The ground is worn-out. If you're looking for a wealthy client, you're chasing ghosts."

"Do you know he's allowing his fields to lie fallow for these two years?"

Greg's face went blank.

George Ridgeway turned away and closed Greg's door very gently.

George caught up with Sling on the street and greeted him. "How about a cup of coffee."

"Sure, George. I probably need to talk to you anyway." Sling was glum and quiet.

"I'm splitting with Greg. It's time I went on my own. John Perez is interested in sharing office space, and we've rented the ground floor of the old Tonner Building. In researching the building...am I to understand that you own it?"

"My granddaddy's. Let me know what you need in renovations, and we'll see to it."

"We'd thought we'd have to see to it ourselves."

"Naw." Sling shook his head. "There's a Trust. We can tap it for such things."

There was a thoughtful silence and finally George mentioned: "Surely you could have gone to college?"

Sling smiled at George. "My life is exactly as I want it. It was very important that the kids grow up the way they did. My dad was stern and told me several times that if he wasn't there, I was to keep the kids under my thumb. He was right. If they hadn't had to work like hell to get where they are today, they'd've been spoiled rotten. Do you remember Kit at all? He was a real handful, and he could charm the pants off any female he wanted. Other than actually going on campus, I had all the means of learning available to me. I can speak any way I want. It's easier for most people to hear me in one way. I have no cause to impress anyone."

"You're badly underestimated."

"No. I live in a community that accepts me as a part of them. That's what's important."

"But everyone thought you were scraping the bottom of the Mueller barrel."

"It was best that way. And we did it all without touching the Trust and without selling an acre. We all walk better because we made it."

"You could hire anyone for this fight for the grandparents' house." George was a little pensive.

"I've hired you."

"When?"

"Just now. You called to me and you didn't know I could afford you. I'll move my files out of Greg's office when you're ready."

George felt a little disoriented.

"The Trust is a trust between us," Sling cautioned. "Greg never knew of it. Most people don't. You didn't. If I hadn't been so disappointed in Greg's conduct, you wouldn't ever have known. You're on your honor."

"Yes."

Sling smiled. "You'll do fine."

The two men shook hands and parted.

When Sling went back by Clovis's house, there was a great big flatbed truck with long poles, and a businesslike mechanical posthole digger. The truck made the house look like a tacky, ill-used toy.

Not surprisingly, Sling pulled into the lane and parked some distance away. He got out of his pickup and stood a while as he surveyed the busy, expertly controlled chaos. Miss Penny was sitting on a porch rocking chair placed off to one side of the yard. She was sewing and watching.

Sling went over to Miss Penny's side and gestured toward the workmen and then frowned.

Miss Penny understood he was puzzled. "She's building a shade for the house."

Sling couldn't think of anything to say. He stood there with his boots planted apart, his fingers in his back pockets and watched.

After a time, Clovis came over and stood beside him.

He asked in a serious voice, "What are you doing?"

"Isn't this exciting?" She laughed.

"What am I paying for here?"

"Nothing." She put a comforting hand on his shoulder and paralyzed him. "I'm fixing up my house. I need shade. It takes a while to grow trees, so I'm making shade."

"How?" He didn't move, so that her hand would stay on his shoulder.

"Eight of the high poles will be placed out from each corner of the house with another planted halfway in between. See?"

He was stunned. She'd put her hand between his arm and body and was holding his arm, and as she gestured, her soft round breast touched his arm. He blinked.

"Oh, silly, it's simple. Here. Let me show you."

She released him! He stood frowning at her.

She took a stick and drew in the dust. "This square is the house, from above." She drew the square. "These will be the poles." She put one at each corner, then another halfway between each corner. "See? Eight poles."

"Yeah."

"Then crossbeams will be attached to all four sides making another square." She drew lines between all

the poles. "But then, tilted cross-boards will be lined
from the east to the west, across the square, like that."

"Why?"

"They'll be tilted so that the roof is shaded from the
evening sun. And since the poles are eight feet out
from the sides of the house, the windows will be
shaded too. The house will be cooler."

"That's clever, Clovis." It was the first time he'd
said her name to her, and he was struck with that.

"You aren't angry?"

He replied solemnly, "It could make pulling the
house down a little harder."

She laughed.

"I need the bill from Sweetie for the plumbing
work."

"No."

"And I'll pay for this." He gestured toward the
chaos.

"No."

He gave her an enduringly patient look and said,
"I'm glad I was never tempted to have rental property. Renters must drive the landlords crazy, if you're
any sample."

She scoffed at that. "You find me stimulating."

"Very." She probably meant his ire and not his
body's response. He stood there, his hands in his
pockets, and his lower lip over his upper lip in a disgruntled way.

She had the nerve to reach up a finger and pull his
lower lip down. "Don't sulk. It'll be wonderful for
Miss Penny and me. The house will be cooler." She
smiled. "They'll dig the postholes for the chicken
fence, too."

"I thought we'd agreed not to have chickens here."

"No."

"I *told* you—"

"I know." She looped her arm through his again and rendered him speechless.

Miss Penny rocked and smiled.

The next day was Sunday and the day of rest. Sling was curious if the Indiana refugee would dare to show her face in a church, and he took pains in dressing. He wore a dark blue suit, a white shirt and a red tie, but he still had on boots and a Stetson. He looked like a darkly dangerous man.

Clovis and Miss Penny came in rather late and sat in back. Sling did some inventive body shifting as the congregation sat or rose to sing, and he kept the pair under observation.

When the service was over, he got to them almost first. That took clever footwork, quick hellos to greeters, and a smooth avoidance of the preacher, who was astonished to see Sling there and had particularly wanted to shake his hand.

Sling slyly invited the ladies to his house for Sunday dinner, hoping for an invitation to her house. And the big surprise was, they accepted his invitation.

While the preacher was greeting the ladies and welcoming them, Sling collared Tom and sent him home to alert Chin that guests were on the way. Tom laughed. Sling pulled him back and growled, "Served family-style. Sunday dinner. Got that?"

"How—"

"Nuke it." Sling's tone was a dire threat, because Chin refused to use a microwave.

"Now—"

But Sling only snarled through his teeth, "Do it!"

Anybody over four with two brain-cells would have understood that. And Sling slammed his truck keys into Tom's hand.

Sling was going to let Tom drive his new pickup! It was like being knighted.

Therefore it was Sling who drove Clovis's car out to the Mueller place. That had surprised her. Of course, she hadn't realized that Sling's invitation was a fake, and Sling had no way of getting back to his place.

Confronted by the limitations of her car, Clovis weighed the solution. If she drove, Miss Penny would have to sit in the mini back seat because there wasn't any way, at all, for Sling to fold himself into that foolishly small space. And for Miss Penny to demand her brittle bones do what they would have to in order to get herself back there was outside reality.

Clovis took a deep breath, handed Sling her keys and slid her supple, adjustable body modestly into that tricky space without turning a hair.

Sling smiled at her. Then he let Miss Penny take all the time she needed to realign her body from standing to sitting, and he saw to it that her seat belt was buckled.

Sling did that with such patience and so automatically, that Clovis understood he was very well practiced in assisting old ladies into cars or trucks. She realized that he had done the same thing—how many times?—for Cousin Eileen.

Clovis didn't know Sling was deliberately delaying in order to give Chin a little time, so she was thoughtful as they drove out to the Mueller place. She watched

Sling as she slowed and directed Miss Penny's attention to a deer that was standing still as a statue, almost indiscernible in the brush about twenty feet back from the road.

He slowed almost to a standstill as a rattler writhed its way across the dusty road. And he rolled down the window so that Miss Penny could exclaim over its camouflage in the dusty, roadside weeds. She said, "Clovis? My glasses are a miracle."

Clovis touched her shoulder in reply, since the lady couldn't hear.

Sling lifted his glance to the rearview mirror and his eyes smiled at Clovis in a benediction that topped the preacher's.

Clovis was surprised by the modesty of the Mueller layout. What had she expected? The big, well-kept barn was expected and the other buildings for equipment were not a surprise. But the simple, one-and-a-half-story, unpainted, Irish flat-house was. It was larger than the roadside proliferation of the early-day shacks. But it did carry that design.

There was a porch across the front, with rocking chairs and a handy railing on which to prop one's feet. The front door led into a large living/dining-room combination with a fireplace. A kitchen was off to one side, behind the dining area. Behind the fireplace was a room used as an office. The hallway led to the bedrooms in the back. This hall had a stairwell to the attic. It had been a dorm for the boys as they grew up.

Sling's guests were greeted at the door by Chin. He wore silk Chinese dress, a round black silk hat and his best enigmatic smile—a little wider than usual. He greeted the ladies with great charm.

The other men were alike in that they had carefully slicked-down hair, and since they always wore hats, they had white foreheads while the lower part of their faces was tanned.

The table was set in the dining room, but it was laid out to include the guests. Two other ranch hands were included. They looked scrubbed and a little frayed by all they'd done in that half hour. Then there was Tom, who wouldn't have missed this meal for anything. He couldn't get rid of his smile. And, of course, there was Chin.

There was a cloth for the table and the best china and flatware. There were rather scraggly field-flowers, hastily gathered, and a meal fit for company.

The menu was a little curious. There was still-icy thawed cranberry relish to go with the brook trout. The vegetables were probably drained soup with a packaged dressing. And the dessert was a whiskey-imbued Christmas fruitcake—a tad crumbly—with brandy sauce. Yes. It was all served with wine and iced tea. And there were demitassees for coffee with that dessert.

They had a hilarious time. The men set themselves to entertain Miss Penny, and they were great mimes. Sometimes they had to leave their chairs in order to demonstrate something specially.

If Miss Culpepper had been there as their lone guest, it would have been an awkward time, she was so breathtaking. But the men were used to old ladies. They sneaked glances at Miss Culpepper and admired her, but they blushed that she was that close to them. They could relax with Miss Penny.

And Miss Penny laughed and laughed. They had to go get her a clean handkerchief so that she could wipe her eyes, which had become wet with laughter. Clovis watched it all and saw them as the people they were.

When Miss Penny was resting on a lounge chair in the shade on the porch, with Spots to guard her, Clovis and Sling strolled out to the barn to see the animals. She had already met Tucker, who made himself present and accounted for, and showed off for Clovis, begging sugar. Sling took her hand and slid a cube into it, taking more time than was needed.

Doing that affected him rather uncomfortably. He wondered if he could sneak her up into the barn loft, which held a year's supply of fresh hay. He gave her a side glance and saw that Tucker amused her.

She inquired, "How did he get so spoiled?"

"I'm glad you understand that. The only one he pulls his dastardly tricks on is me. If you would like to ride him, he'd be a gentleman."

"No, thanks."

"Don't set your mind against him. We'll see."

Then, when the guests were ready to leave, Sling instructed Clovis in his commands to Spots, and he told the dog to guard them. Sling opened Clovis's car door and told the dog to get into the back seat and go along.

Spots stared in disbelief. He did get into the car, and Clovis drove away. Spots looked out the back window for a while, then he turned his back on Sling.

Sling sighed. What a man had to do to get a woman's attention was really a chore. He wished the next couple of weeks gone so that he could get down to some seriously friendly moves.

He told the hands, "You guys were great. You were nice to our guests. Thank you. The table was pretty. The food was an interesting mix. Brilliant."

That brought hoots and raucous laughs.

Sling went on: "You were very kind to Miss Penny. I appreciate that."

And Pedro said, "We haven't yet gotten ptomaine!"

While the men laughed and dispersed, Sling went up into the attic and watched Clovis's little car reach home. He could see the chicken house quite well. And the beginnings of her weird shade solutions. It was going to be a little eccentric, but it could be quite practical. He would contrive to mention the oaks that Lizzie had cut down.

The construction of the rather ponderous shade solution took several days. Since it was his land and he had to impress that fact on everyone, Sling was present. He offered suggestions and was mostly ignored.

During the day, as the men worked, people from the area stopped by to watch. It was something different, something to talk about. And more people came by. They reserved their opinions of the shade solution.

Sling warned Clovis: "Some evening when this is done, you're going to have to have a roof party and let them experience this, you know. It'll be very interesting to have that slatted shade over the house. You'll have to limit the guest list. Can't have too many people up there at a time."

"Of course. Who is the judge who will hear our case?"

Sling squinted at Clovis. "You gonna invite him? You're a wily, underhanded woman."

She gave him a glance that almost lifted the hair off his head. Was it a trick of the light? Did she mean to flirt with him? How could a man tell?

He told her, "I've been elected to escort you and Miss Penny to the square dance on Saturday. Will you allow that?"

"I might." She was a little snippy, but her lips weren't narrowed or tight. He decided she didn't mind him escorting her, and he carried that thought around like a pretty seashell to be taken out and admired.

Clovis was just delighted as the work progressed. When the workers quit for the day, she would go up on the roof and look around.

On the third evening, she even invited Sling into the house and up to the roof to inspect the progress. The beams were twelve feet above the flat roof. There was still the feeling of space and openness.

She danced on the tarp, still there from the sprinkle weeks before, and she hugged herself.

He could have done that for her.

Then she got her flute out and played it for him. It wasn't actually for him. She simply played, and he happened to be there.

It *was* the mystery sound. It was a low, sweet sound, not the intrusive, relentlessly reedy flute prerequisite to all nature shows on television. Her flute wove with the sounds of the wind and grasses, but it spoke of the sea.

She perched up on the railing and lost herself in the sound, and Sling stood by her to catch her if she should begin to fall. He thought she was careless of herself, and she dismayed him.

But one good thing happened. As they were there and she was playing, a car drove into the yard, and Spots wouldn't let the driver out of the car. The intruder had been Greg, her lawyer.

Sling didn't whistle the dog off, and Clovis was concentrated on her music and unaware. With great satisfaction, Sling watched Greg's car leave.

When, the next day, Clovis said to Sling, "Did you see Greg come by last night?"

"Was he here? What time was that?"

"I believe it must have been while we were on the roof. He said Spots wouldn't let him out of the car."

"Well," said Sling carefully. "He's always been good about keeping varmints at bay."

"Sling," she chided him. But she laughed.

Sling slipped the dog some tidbits.

And later that week in town, when someone taunted Sling, "What's your dog doing over at Miss Culpepper's?" Sling turned his head slowly and stared. Then he said in a level voice, "Keeping the coyotes away."

No one else mentioned the dog again. At least not to Sling.

Six

The posthole digger did the trench and holes for the chicken fence. Sturdy posts were inserted into the holes and made to stand solid. That was done over Sling's dead body. He objected to the last breath, but Clovis wasn't at all impressed.

The men were willing to listen to Sling and they did, as he intruded and objected. But Clovis just patted his chest as she linked arms with him, which paralyzed him into silence. She told them to go ahead. Unable to speak, Sling was silent. The workers did go ahead.

When she released Sling and he recovered his wits, he growled at her. "You've got to be the only woman in all Christendom that's this stubborn."

She smiled. "'In all Christendom'? You read!"

"And write." He was annoyed.

"You're a romantic!"

He stared at her and thought she might have some smarts, after all, if she realized that she made him feel romantic.

But she didn't take him down to the creek bed, into the bushes and assuage his passions. She went back to the work at hand.

She directed that the machine dig four holes and put in posts to raise the chicken house several feet up off the ground. Then the machine dug two other, rather larger holes, but they were left empty.

Clovis had designed the enclosure to circle the eccentric chicken shelter. She had gravel brought and most was spread on the lane but a little was put in the chicken area.

When all the men got into the various trucks and left, Clovis looked at the changes and was satisfied.

"What goes in those holes, there?" Sling asked.

"Trees."

"For the chickens?" He couldn't believe that.

"I have shade, they should, too."

"You're very strange and different."

Sassily, she agreed. "From you."

He knew. He knew. "Do you know Lizzie had some great oaks cut down from around the house?"

She looked around and mused softly: "I wonder why."

"We never did know." He regarded her for a time, then reminded her: "You do recall that you've agreed to allow me to escort you and Miss Penny to the square dance on Saturday?"

"Why, I believe I did." She acted rather elaborately startled.

"You're to wear your fullest skirt and that red petticoat you keep bragging about." He grinned. "I said I'd deliver you two, being as how I'm right here and you are living on my property."

"How kind and neighborly."

"Miss Culpepper, do you realize what happens to sassy females?"

"No."

"Just keep it up, and you'll find out."

The chicken wire couldn't be delivered until the next week. And without some project to supervise, Sling didn't know how to excuse his prolonged presence there.

But he didn't seem to be able to stay on his own place, either. He visited a lot. He made the rounds of just about everybody so many times that it caught their attention. "Why's Sling so restless?" "Maybe it's going to be his turn to go off for a while."

And Fredricka told Clovis, "You're just lucky this is a square dance on Saturday. Sling insists on escorting you and Miss Penny, and he can't dance worth a darn. He squashes a woman up against him and just shuffles. I know that sounds lascivious and exciting, but it's only that he doesn't know how to dance. And he talks about stomach worms in horses and breeding bulls and exciting things like that."

"He can't dance?"

"He manages pretty well in square dancing, and you change partners a lot, so it isn't as bad."

"He squashes you?"

"All the women," Fredricka agreed. "They love it."

"Oh."

It was such a tiny "Oh" but Fredricka heard it. And she thought: Hmm. So Miss Culpepper's attention had been caught by the notoriously dangerous-looking Sling? That would never do. Poor Clovis would just be snared inadvertently by a noninterested Sling, and her heart would be broken. Of all people, Fredricka knew about Sling. He was a hollow facade of allure. She said to Clovis, "Sling isn't interested in women."

"What!"

"Oh." Fredricka flopped a hand. "I know he looks dangerous as sin and as tempting, but he only looks that way." And having saved Clovis from breaking her heart uselessly, Fredricka added, "He's an outdoor man and he's really only comfortable talking to men. Women have always found him fascinating, but he's never learned to flirt or flatter. He's incapable of just male-female conversation, teasing and being easy. With the way he looks so dark and dangerous, you'd think he'd be exciting for a woman. I know it's a shame, but it just isn't so. See you Saturday at the square dance. You'll get to meet all those other men who aren't nailed down."

Clovis used the word again: "Oh." She was rather distracted and pensive.

That night her music was yearning as she sent it across over the rise to Sling who lay in bed and listened, sure that she wanted him...or somebody. Why not him?

But she was a little cool when Sling came by for them Saturday evening. She did notice that while he automatically gave Miss Penny his hand and helped her down the front steps, he watched Clovis as he told

Miss Penny, "I would carry you down these stairs, but then if someone saw that, they'd think we were eloping, and you have to know I'm too young for you."

Miss Penny couldn't hear his nonsense. He was teasing Clovis.

With practiced ease, he set a worn, wooden step on the ground so that Miss Penny could mount up to the cab of his pickup without any strain. He helped Clovis, too, and he put his hand on the small of her back as if she were more fragile than Miss Penny. He said to her, "So, you brazen woman, you actually did wear that red petticoat!"

She waited until he went around the truck, got in and settled in the driver's seat before she replied, "Now, how could you know I'm wearing my red petticoat?" And she was again aware that they could talk quite easily past Miss Penny sitting there between them, and not watch their words at all.

"I saw that wicked garment peek out from under your hem, and I am shocked, Miss Culpepper. I had no idea you were a flirt who would swish her skirts around and be seductive. You want to set all these poor lonesome cowboys on their very ears?"

"You *told* me to wear it!"

"I thought surely you would realize I was testing you. And there you are, sitting over there with your hot bottom on that shameless red skirt."

That sounded like man-woman teasing to Clovis. Wasn't it? But she'd been warned off and she wasn't sure how to respond.

As they drove along in silence, he said, "No complaints? Your unknown-to-you cousin, who was a *burr* to us all, always mentioned something disparaging about my trucks. Sometimes it was the same criticism each time in one day.''

That was revealing. Her distant cousin Eileen not only was a constant complainer, but she would make him drive her somewhere several times in one day. Clovis was thoughtful.

The smell of ham slowly, insidiously filled the cabin of the pickup. ''Is that ham?''

''Excellent sense of smell.'' He complimented her. ''We're going to have a supper that would stun an ordinary race of people into a stupor, but us Texans can handle a little thing like that. You, being a Yankee, should take it easy on the food until you become acclimatized.''

''Were we supposed to bring something? I am embarrassed.''

''No. You're my guest. I provide the food. But, I would like to ask if you will pretend it's yours. You see—''

''It's only half-baked,'' she guessed.

''No, it's a fully baked, Virginia ham. A Texas pig, but it's called a Virginia ham. No, don't strain over that. Figure it out in your idle time.''

She fretted. ''I could have brought something if you'd only told me.''

''No, no, no. You're a guest this time. After this, you have to bring your best dish and show off like all the ladies do.''

''Grandmother's Spode?'' She grinned at him.

He laughed. ''No. Not a china dish. Food. But you will do it? Pretend this is your ham?''

''Why should I do that?''

"Well, you see, a while back Chin was in the hospital for a couple of days—with ptomaine."

She laughed first, then said, "Oh."

"He's having a terrible time of it. Somebody let the cat out of the bag and the word spread. You should hear the hands at *every meal* making Chin take the first bite and watching him in all sorts of extravagant poses. It's really funny. Then Chin does his inscrutable Chinese bit and tastes the food."

She grinned.

"After everybody's eaten something, Chin falls to the floor."

"Who writes your material?"

"I'm only telling the facts, ma'am."

Then Sling explained the dance would be at the Hall at Coopers' field. "All our dances are there. The Hall's a little plain, but we have a good time. The ladies won't allow booze in the building, but I have some here in the truck. Tell Miss Penny she's not to overindulge, but you can."

"You like drunken women?"

"I like pliant ones."

That confused Clovis. If he liked pliant women, he must not talk cattle-and-horse ailments all of the time.

The Hall was plain. Plain? It was a windowless rectangle with a high roof braced with metal struts like a plane hangar. It was probably one of the ugliest buildings Clovis had ever seen.

But she soon forgot that. Everyone was welcoming and the place was noisy. Instead of a little-bitty dance floor, the whole center was open and the tables had been pushed over to the edges.

First, they ate. There were the usual "Oh, your salad was marvelous" and the response: "Was it really? I didn't think it was quite up to par," and "Nobody can beat my salads." "Where did you find this recipe? It's very...unusual." But everyone ate the ham and complimented Clovis.

"What if they all get sick?" she whispered to Sling.

"Nobody will ever ask you to bring anything else— if it's narrowed down to the ham. But in this mob, they'll never know. It's just important that Chin's reputation stays inside the family."

She snubbed him. "I'm not of your family."

And he retorted wickedly, "You live on my land."

The whole evening was fun. Clovis had to learn how to square dance, and Sling was a lighthearted teacher. He wouldn't allow anyone else to instruct her. They made a lot of mistakes because his attention wasn't concentrated on his feet.

He was the instigator for one round of round dancing.

"Round dance?"

"Yeah. It's just one couple each and they dance 'round."

"Ahhh." And she wondered with whom he wanted to dance "all squashed up," as Fredricka had mentioned.

He danced with Clovis, and he wouldn't allow anyone to cut in. It was just like Fredricka had warned, because Clovis loved being squashed against Sling.

However, he didn't talk about the ailments of cattle and horses. He told her, "You need to wear a brassiere."

Clovis had never before in her life heard anyone say the whole word. Her breasts were part of what was squashed against him. Indignantly, she said, "I do not bounce. I'm not that... We will not discuss my... chest."

He held her very tightly and barely shuffled as he looked off into the crowd. "You jiggle."

"I do not, either."

"Well, not exactly, but your chests shiver along and the men look at you and their hands curl."

"Good grief!"

"I knew you didn't know."

She took a deep breath and said, "Hah!"

He groaned.

"What's the matter?"

"Don't breathe."

"I have to breathe. What's your problem?"

"Everything on me is uncurled and standing out straight."

"What?"

Very seriously, he looked down into her face without loosening his death grip on her body, and he explained, "My chest hair has uncrinkled and is standing out rigid, just like everything else."

Her head was back and his was tilted down over hers so that their eyes were only about three inches apart. She said, "Oh."

"I figure you owe me a minimum of thirty dollars a week in rent."

"You want a new cook?"

"Not hardly. I've got Chin."

"As I recall, he's the cook who was hospitalized for ptomaine?"

"Yeah. But after thirty-four years, I've built up an immunity. We need to discuss ways for you to pay your rent on that section of my land."

As their long, long, mesmerized look continued, she said, "It's mine."

That caught his attention and he was almost distracted from the feel of her body so close against his. "You claiming the whole ranch?"

"No. That corner."

He slowly shook his head. His face serious, his grip unrelenting, all of his body muscles were rigid. "You can't just live there free. That's not civilized."

And she smiled just a little. "But you are?"

"Yeah."

"I can't breathe very well."

"You shouldn't at all. When you do, men look at your chest."

"I never noticed that. You must be mistaken."

"I watch."

"Why?"

"I don't like other men watching your chest."

"Why?" This time her lips formed the word differently, slower.

"You're under my protection. I'm responsible for you."

Her lashes lowered. She said a disappointed "Oh."

"If anybody gets your goodies, it's gonna be me."

Her widened eyes looked at his again. "You're not supposed to talk that way."

"I'm supposed to be sly and devious?"

"Of course!"

It was his turn to say "Oh." He shuffled a little bit without saying anything, hardly moving any distance. "One of the nice things about Miss Penny being deaf is that she won't hear me shrieking as you chase me around your house tonight."

"Why am I going to chase you?"

"To corrupt my morals."

"I see. Why am I going to do that?"

"Because you're curious about me, and you wonder if I'm a good lover."

"Why, Mr. Mueller! How you do go on!"

"You feel so good against my body." He groaned softly in agony. "I'm just about to go crazy."

"If you did something like that right here, what would people say?"

He was positive. "They'll look at you in censure because you've kept me dangling so long."

"Have you been out to the liquor stash in your truck?"

"No," he assured her. "I'm cold sober and very needy."

"You need . . . a drink?"

"A taste of you."

"How can you be so fresh?" she scolded. "We are barely ac—"

"Not yet."

"Now, now. We are bare—"

"Pretty soon," he promised. "We can't strip right here in the middle of the Hall. People would *talk,* and we can't have that." He turned his wrist and looked at his watch. "It's too early even to leave here. We'll have to be brave."

"I'm not leaving this Hall with you," she decided.

"Why not?"

"If I did, you'd think I was just asking you to . . ."

He asked, "Make love to you?"

"Yes."

"Ah. You said 'Yes', so you agree."

She sputtered. "No. I didn't mean—"

"You didn't mean it?" He was shocked. "Now, I never thought you'd be a tease. Shame on you, leading a nice boy like me along thataway."

And she relaxed. He was teasing. She grinned and tried to move back from his death grip, but he only tightened his arms. "Don't move. I'll lose count of the steps."

That only made her laugh.

And he groaned and put his head down by hers.

Sling instigated one other slow dance. The only other man in the place who was brave enough to counter Sling's possessiveness was Moose. He was coming over in a dead line, and Sling said, "That's Moose."

"He's big enough."

"Yeah," Sling warned. "He's wild and woolly and full of fleas."

"Fleas?"

"It's the truth. By this time, they're his old friends. He's named them all."

Moose came up and looked down into Sling's eyes. "How're you, Sling?"

"Fine. How're Mike, Jim, Rosco, the rest?"

Those men were Moose's hands on his place. But with the lead-in about fleas, it sounded to Clovis that they were talking about his private collection of body fleas.

Moose beamed. "Fine. Fine."

"Mitzie?" The foreman's wife.

"Just the same. She got them all under control." Moose laughed. "You know Mitzie."

"Only from a distance." Sling smiled.

Moose nodded. "Best that way. I hear she's pregnant."

"Nice. You need some more little ones around." Sling slid a glance at Clovis.

Clovis's skin began to itch and she was biting her lower lip.

"I'd like an introduction to the little lady."

Clovis thought Moose was like a minor character out of an early John Wayne movie.

Sling said, "Melvin, I'd like you to meet Clovis Culpepper."

"So you're Moose." She smiled up at the big man.

"Who told you that?"

"Sling." She slid an amused glance at Sling, expecting him to blanch.

But Moose said, "Oh. Well, he can."

"Because he's a bully?" She gave Sling another side look.

"Naw, we respect him."

"Why?"

Sling frowned in mock offense. "Now, how come you ask that?"

Moose said, "I meant to ask you to dance, Miss Culpepper, but I can see that Sling still has some work to do on you. I'll wait till you're safer."

Clovis gasped, but Sling snorted in barely controlled laughter. He said, "Glad you understand."

Moose said, "No wonder you've been out and running all over the country. A little restless?"

"Careful."

"I hear." Moose held up his great hands and backed away.

The rest of the evening was one long square dance. It was loud and there was laughter, and Clovis had a marvelous time. Sling never let her out of his control. He blocked and gave looks and caught arms. She was his for as long as it took.

There were some earnest contenders. One was Greg Thompson, and he particularly never managed to get close. He got set up in a square so that he'd swing Clovis and occasionally partner her, but at the last minute, Sling switched with another couple and moved Clovis into another set. Sling made no bones about his possession. It was the talk of the Hall.

In the ladies' room. Fredricka grinned at Clovis. "No talk of breeding problems?"

And Clovis laughed and blushed, shaking her head.

Fredricka looked thoughtful.

As the evening lengthened, Miss Penny dozed in a chair near some other old ladies. It was a good excuse for Sling to tell Clovis they really ought to take Miss Penny home. It was past her bedtime.

So the three exited from the Hall, and since the old lady was along, there were no catcalls or sly remarks. With Miss Penny between them, they drove toward the grandparents' house. Miss Penny nodded off, and Clovis put her arm around their chaperone leaning the old head on her soft shoulder.

As they drove through the night, Sling would glance aside to see that tender scene. So he didn't see the deer until too late, and it crashed into the pickup, up onto the hood and shattered the windshield!

Clovis held Miss Penny safely and the killing hoof intruded where her head would have been. Sling was out of the truck and around to their door, opening it. "Are you all right?"

"What happened?" Miss Penny's frail voice was alarmed.

"We hit a deer," Sling signaled. "Are you both okay?"

"Yes," Clovis said quickly. "Sling, are you all right?"

There was blood on them. Theirs? "Yeah. I shoulda been watching."

"I don't think you could have missed it. It came so suddenly. You were braking even as I first saw it."

But he'd been looking at her.

He touched the blood on her face and her shoulder. "Are you really all right?"

"Yes."

With that assurance, Sling got the ladies out. They stood by the wayside, watching. Still shocked.

Sling wrested the carcass from the hood and windshield, pulled it over the cab roof and onto the truck bed.

He cleaned the shattered glass off the seat and floor, then helped the ladies back into the cab of the pickup.

"Are you two really okay?"

"Yes."

"Here's a blanket. With the windshield gone, it'll be a little cool."

He took them home. There he reassured an alert Spots, who smelled the blood. Sling helped the women from the truck and up onto the porch. Miss Penny went inside.

Sling took Clovis very gently into his arms to hold her, and he kissed her. He held her tenderly. It wasn't as he'd held her to dance. It was different, cherishing. He groaned, "My God, I thought I'd killed you."

Her voice trembled. "I saw the windshield break around you and—"

"I know."

"Don't leave. I need to see if Miss Penny is all right. I'll be down in a minute."

"Be sure she isn't cut or hurt. I'll wait here."

Sling used her phone to call a family he knew who could use the meat and skin of the deer. He was hanging up when Clovis came back downstairs. He watched her. "Is she okay?"

"She really is. She regrets the deer, but we're both amazed none of us was hurt. If she hadn't been asleep..."

"If we'd been alone, you would have been sitting next to me. Are you sure you're all right?"

"I really am."

She had washed the deer's blood from her face and hands. There were no cuts. He held her against him and he trembled. "Thank God."

She was so moved by him that a tear formed. She leaned against him and sighed.

"I have to take the deer to a family I know. I'll help them skin it and cut it up. It's a big job. I'll be a while. You ought to get to bed. I'll see you tomorrow."

"We'll be going to church."

"Sit with me?"

She was hesitant. To sit with a man in church was something of a declaration in an area as sparse as that.

"Don't be a coward." His voice was husky and very low.

She laughed in her throat. "How like the area's confirmed bachelor to put a temporary brand on the new woman in the area."

"One does as one must."

He'd quoted that so readily that he must have heard it many times from someone. She smiled and said, "All right. We'll see you in church."

He kissed her differently then. He did it with skill and passion, just about blowing off the tops of their heads. His breathing changed, his muscles tensed, his body reacted to her and he trembled. "I want you so bad that . . ." He groaned softly.

And she responded. She seemed to become breathless and a little feverish. She leaned into him and stretched up his body and put her arms around his shoulders as she kissed him back.

"You were the prettiest girl there, do you know that? And that red petticoat has got to be moth-balled. Or you can wear it in the house, just for me. To see that flip as you danced, any man would know you're a woman who needs taking."

"Oh?"

"But you're not allowing any man anywhere near you, hear me? Only me."

He kissed her again. And the kiss was different yet again. It demanded that she fly with him. He spun her senses and moved his hard hands as he molded her against his hard body deliciously. "You're driving me crazy."

She whispered, "I'm not doing anything."

"You're breathing and your arms are around me and your soft body is along mine. Kiss me. Let me know you realize I'm a man."

With that, he slid his hard hands down her back and pulled her body against the need of him. She got a little dizzy.

He held her up and gave her no quarter. He just kissed her again. What a wicked way he had. And Fredricka said Sling was a man's man and didn't care for women? Fredricka had been badly misled. No man could kiss that way if he didn't really, *really* like women. And he craved her. That was apparent.

Would she allow that?

How could she not? She had been fascinated by him from the first time she'd walked across that yard and told him he could have the branded furniture—when she'd finished with it.

He'd just watched her. He hadn't changed expression or gotten mad or done anything. He'd watched her eyes and she'd been hard-pressed not to fling herself at him. She'd been magnificent in her control.

Where was it now?

He said, "I'd like to put you right down here on the floor and show you how to pay your rent, but I haven't time right now. I'll have to get back to you. Behave until I can take control over you again. Hear me?"

And her floppy neck nodded her head. Where *was* the aloof Miss Culpepper? Nowhere around.

He patted her fanny in a very familiar manner, kissed her until her cheeks were flushed with sexual heat, and he left her there.

He didn't walk too well, but he did get out to his injured pickup, and he blinked the lights as he drove slowly from her yard.

On the road, he slowed, and she could see that he watched her shadow in the doorway. She couldn't move. He blinked the lights again. Then he drove again.

There had been no words of love. Only of need.

Seven

On Sunday morning when Miss Penny and Clovis came out the door onto the porch, they were greeted silently by Spots. And they found Sling on their front porch. He, too, was dressed for church. He was sitting on one of the rockers, tilted back with his booted feet on the railing. His big hands were folded on his flat stomach, his Stetson was tilted down over his eyes and he was sound asleep.

The two women stood looking at him for a while, then they smiled at each other, tiptoed off the porch, down the steps and went quietly to the car. They noted he had driven a ratty old pickup. His new pickup would have to be repaired. They got into Clovis's white car, she started it carefully, and they eased away.

He was still sleeping an hour later when they returned. Spots greeted them, glad to see them and laughed at them but he didn't bark. The women petted him and waited until he had finished his greeting. Then they went back up onto the porch.

Again the two women stood and watched Sling sleep before they went carefully into the house and up the stairs to change into cooler clothing. In shorts and a loose top, Clovis came down barefooted and went to the kitchen to make lemonade.

She carried an ice-tinkling glass out to the porch. From under his hat, Sling said, "Put a little gin in mine."

"You missed church."

"God knows what all I had to do last night."

To show that she also knew, she told him, "You helped butcher that deer."

"I had to leave you here, relatively untouched, in order to do that."

"Oh?" She encouraged him to elaborate.

"That made me suffer all night long."

"I didn't sleep very well, either."

He lifted the hat to look up at her. "You wanted me in your bed."

"I kept seeing that deer hoof inches from your head."

"You didn't want me hurt."

She moved her shoulders and tilted her head. Then she lied, moving her hands and assuming a prissy expression, "I was so shaken that I couldn't remember how to drive a pickup with gears, and I doubted if Miss Penny could handle gears at all."

His eyes bored into her like flames and he growled the words. "You're an asinine woman. I think it was frustrated men who ran you out of Indiana in that red petticoat.''

"You were sleeping so hard."

"I heard you leave. I thought you'd probably be so grateful, to still be whole today, that you'd say enough prayers for us both."

"I was well out of range of being hurt by the deer."

"Because of the deer," he explained as to a backward child, "you slept alone last night."

"What makes you so sure that you'd have been in my bed?''

"What makes you think for a minute that I wouldn't have been?''

He was different. He rather unsettled her. This was a dangerous man. If she had no intentions of leading him along until he took her, she should stop him now. This was her last chance. She smiled just a little. "I probably would have been so loud—in my objections, sir—that Miss Penny's hearing would have been restored." She widened her eyes, smiled and lifted her hands up to illustrate the miracle.

Watching her like the chancy animal he was, he warned her, "You know you're flirting on the edge of my limits?''

In a snooty snub, she retorted, "In my youth, I practiced as a tightrope walker."

"And you never lost your balance?''

"The rope was only a foot above the ground."

"You're a mile high on this rope, lady, and you'd better have a parachute."

She didn't back off. "You don't scare me."

He didn't reply. He just looked at her, but his breathing changed.

Busily she said, "Will you stay for dinner? We have a pot roast in the oven, with carrots, potatoes and onions. There'll be a fruit salad, and Miss Penny is only now making a chocolate cake. Does that tempt you?"

"What if I choose another dessert?"

"If you prefer apple pie, say so right now."

"I want you."

"You can try. You've promised me you're not a ravisher. So you'll have to convince me. I am tempted."

"Not the pie. Just give me a bite of Eden's Apple."

"Ahhh. You know about the Snake in The Garden."

His breath was a little quicker. "What did he whisper to you?" And his tone urged her to flirt seriously.

"Not a word." She replied conversationally. "The message I had was from you. You hinted how I could pay the rent."

"If you call that a hint, what sort of words do I have to use?"

"I'll listen." She folded her hands and assumed a judgmental look.

"Take off your clothes."

She shook her head chidingly. "If that's your technique, no wonder you're still not married."

"I'm about to die for need of your kiss. My soul's parched."

"Now, that's much, much better."

"Well?"

She leaned over quickly, gave him a quick kiss on his forehead and was out of reach before he could react.

He lunged, and she jumped farther back, out of reach, laughing.

He said wickedly, "Your days are numbered. It could even be minutes."

"Help, help!"

"You're pretty sassy for a woman whose chaperon is stone-deaf."

"You would assault me?" She made her eyes big and put one hand across her breasts.

"If that's what it takes."

"I have to go cut up the fruit for the salad."

He lay back in the chair, watching her, his eyes lazy and wicked. There was just the tiniest smile on his lips. He was a patient hunter. He said, "Come here and kiss me improperly."

She smiled and shook her head in tiny little shakes.

"I'll keep my hands on the arms of the chair. Just like this. Come sit on my lap and kiss me one nice squishy kiss."

"You'll keep your hands on the arms of the *chair?* Promise?"

"Come over here."

She hesitated, smiling, then moved a little closer, acting as if she were ready to jump back. Then she sat carefully on his lap and his breathing was fast. She had to lie along his body to reach his mouth, and she kissed him. He pulled up his shoulder to brace her head, and his kiss was a scandal! He kept his hands on the chair arms as he'd promised, but he made the hungriest sounds that were enflaming.

She pushed slowly away from him, and he allowed that. She sat up woozily and held her head, and he watched her avidly. But he kept his promise. She got off his lap, bracing one hand on his iron stomach, and she wobbled to the door. She looked back at him very seriously, then she quietly went inside and carefully closed the screen door.

When he was called in to dinner, he had removed his boots and left them on the porch. He'd put his Stetson on the rocker. That way, anyone coming up on the porch knew who was there and that he was being that casually "at home" in Clovis's house. His house.

At the table and in front of the deaf Miss Penny, he continued his campaign. He mentioned to Clovis: "Lizzie was a cranky, fault-finding woman. That genetic?"

"I'm darling."

"You sure enough look good, but you have to remember that I've had the caretaking of a disagreeable old woman for a lot of years. I need to know what I'm getting into here."

"What sort of certification would you accept?"

"A close relationship?"

"I could lure you in and be another Lizzie before you realized what was happening."

"Well, you ought to do what you can. Mama always said that to our little ones. There was a passel."

"Any of your own?"

"No. Mama and Daddy liked each other. I was the oldest. After they died, I was in charge."

"I would bet you were a tyrant."

"That's a fair description."

"What happened to your parents?"

"Do you know what a norther is? It's a storm that comes in out of that direction. A blue norther is a wicked storm and can cause real damage. In the winter, the sleet and snow and bitter winds drive the cattle before it. They pile up in ravines and against fences and they die.

"The parents were out for an overnight. There were too many of us at home for them ever to have a minute to theirselves. There was a surprise norther. Something spooked my dad's horse. It must have been sudden and a complete surprise, because my dad was thrown.

"The horse went down a gully. It was bad hurt and one of its legs was horrifically broken. Mama shot him. She'd cut the saddle off for the blanket and lugged that and the saddle back up to where Dad was. He didn't die right away. She'd splinted his leg and arm. There was snow in the wrappings, so the norther had hit while she was struggling. She'd covered him with everything, including herself." Sling's voice roughened. "We never found her horse." He rubbed his face with both hands very hard. Then in an almost-normal voice, he said, "I still miss them."

Clovis said, "Damn."

"Yeah."

"So it was just you and the other kids and Chin?"

"No. By then we had three ladies living with us."

"Well, thank goodness for that."

He gave her an ironic look. "They were as old or older than Lizzie. They'd been like Miss Penny. We'd tried to get Lizzie a companion several times, but she was such a hellcat that no one could live with her. We couldn't send them back to the Home. So we moved each failure over to our place. They crept around and dusted, they did a little mending and they played bridge. All us kids are good bridge players. We had to take turns taking the fourth hand.''

Clovis studied Sling as he took his first piece of chocolate cake. With his story, she knew so much about him. About his family. Just that they couldn't take the rejected ladies back to the Home told enough of the family. And they had been committed to Lizzie's care, so they did it. The Muellers were good people.

Did she want only an affair with Sling?

He chewed as he contemplated her. And right there in front of the deaf chaperon, he told Clovis, ''You could help me to be a calm, contented man.''

''By being convenient?''

''Yeah. After all, you're occupying part of my land. Why couldn't I occasionally occupy a part of you? It'd be a fair exchange.''

Clovis's eyes sparkled but she blushed.

He smiled at her, his eyes hot and wicked as he licked his lips slowly.

She glanced at Miss Penny. That lady was daintily eating a little of the cake. She was serene. ''How can you conduct this salacious flirtation in front of such a fragile maiden lady?''

He shook his head once in denial and said quite blandly, ''I'm being quite circumspect. I haven't begun to get graphic.''

She gasped.

He loved it and his chuckle was naughty.

They helped clear the table and put things away. And Miss Penny excused herself to go take a little nap.

Clovis washed the dishes, and Sling dried them. As he walked back and forth, putting a dish in the cupboard and returning to the sink for another, he wondered out loud: "How do you suppose Lizzie ever got entrenched in this house?"

Clovis replied, "A clue to the legitimacy of my claim is that she was deliberately housed here. That's proven by all the Mueller furniture that was *given* to her."

"Don't push your luck," he cautioned. "Why she was here just baffles me. There is a sultry, pouty picture of her as a young woman, long, long ago. But I know full well that she wasn't a mistress to my grandfather, who was a peer. Do you suppose it was my great-grandpaw? I've heard he was wild and woolly, but I would never think he'd be so bold, in those days, as to set up a woman on his own land, this way."

"No one ever found out how she came to live here?"

"Nope. But I know about you. You know the rules for your staying here, and you're taking my suggestions very well."

"I'm not taking them at all." She gave him a snooty look.

"Then how else do you plan to pay your rent?"

She licked her lips, and he watched that, fascinated. She raised her eyebrows and told him, "If by some weird quirk of corrupted law, I should lose my claim, the telephone poles would more than pay the accrued rent. That isn't even mentioning the chicken yard."

"I don't want telephone poles."

"You'll love them."

"I want to love you."

"Explain how you'd go about doing that."

"Well, there'd be some kissing." He put down his towel and showed her how that would be.

She acknowledged: "You do that quite well."

"These kinds of kisses would be different."

"Oh? In what way?"

"More...serious." He kissed her with great skill and temptation. "And there'd be hugging."

"Hold it." She put up a delaying hand.

"I was only showing you."

"Oh."

He explained: "So the hugging wouldn't be... prim."

"I see."

He lifted his head to look at her. "'See'? What do you mean, 'see'? You're supposed to feel."

"You are."

"I'm only demonstrating and instructing."

"You're not being fresh?"

"Not yet," he assured her. "When we get this arrangement set up, I'd be doing you a favor, coming over to your place. That costs you extra, in that you wouldn't get as much rent credit. And if the weather's bad, you, of course, would come to my place."

The lights in her eyes danced. "You can't be out in bad weather?"

"No."

"How nice Texas weather is so perfect."

He nodded agreeably. "It's something to be grateful about, that's true, but we do on occasion have excessive heat or storms and floods. That sort of thing."

"And on those occasions, I'm to take an umbrella and come cross-country?"

He complimented her. "You got it just right."

"Are there any other rules?"

"You're to be on call constantly."

"How would you get anything done at your place?"

He smiled with such humor. "You forget we have the place lying fallow for these two years."

"And you've nothing to do?"

"Nothing else."

And she laughed.

He dried the pots and pans, and they finished up in companionable silence. He reached around her, brushing her breasts. He kissed the back of her neck. And she found dishwashing had taken on a sensual dance of pleasure.

Since he was in stocking feet and she was barefooted, they were needlessly silent as he led her into the front room, closed the door and locked it. He took her over to the soft, plush, Victorian vapors couch.

She allowed that.

He was soberly serious as he very slowly undid the buttons on her loose blouse and pulled it from her shoulders. He hadn't known if she would protest, but she did not. Then he said, "Do me," as he pulled his shirttail from his slacks.

Her fingers trembled a little and she bit her lip as she undid his buttons. His heart was touched by that. She wasn't a skilled lover, used to a man. Her face, too, was serious. He became quite tender with her.

She had to reach up to take off his shirt from his wide shoulders, so he turned and helped with that. In the heat he wore no undershirt and his chest was bare with hairy swirls. She put out her hand to feel his chest, and his body was thrilled by her doing just that.

He removed her bra and looked at her naked breasts. He saw, too, that she blushed, and he leaned down to kiss her soft nipples gently. One hand cupped her as his other hand went to her back to pull her against him. His breathing was harsh. And his body shivered in tiny tremors of desire.

He sat to take off his socks, then stood to unzip his trousers and remove them and his briefs. He did that quite naturally and unselfconsciously. His attention was on her. He saw her look at his sex quite seriously, her lips parted, her breathing quick and shallow.

He undid her shorts and squatted to pull them off her as she lifted her feet one at a time. Balanced, sitting on his heels, his knees wide, he relished the look of her, naked before him. He tsked once, turning his head in a quick almost-shake, and he said, "My, but you're a sight. I don't think you ought to wear clothes."

"Miss Penny would be shocked." Her voice was quick and a little thin.

She was nervous. He slowed himself to take more time with her. He laid her on the armless, backless curled sofa and lay beside her. Her eyes were wide and her mouth soft. He kissed her long and skillfully, tasting her. His hands moved on her with sweet pleasure, pleasuring her.

Her eyelids became heavy and her movements were slow and sensual. She made little sounds that uncrinkled his chest hair, too. He groaned.

In a whisper, she asked, "What's the matter?"

"I hurt."

"What? You hurt?"

"Yeah." His voice was husky. "Give me your hand."

"Well, no wonder! You have a terrible problem there."

"You can help. That's the object of this whole campaign. You are the only one who gets me this way, and the only one who can cure me."

She made a scoffing sound.

"It's true." He rubbed her hand on him and shuddered. "I really need you."

"Show me how to help you."

So he put on a condom and he showed her. She opened to him and accepted his careful invasion very seriously. He was shivering and sweating and panting. He was so disturbed that she was sobered entirely. As his sex was completely sheathed inside her, his sound was of exquisite pain, and her hands were tender on his shoulders and her fingers slipped into his hair to comfort him. Her lips were sweet on his, and they parted as his own demanded that.

His kisses, then, were deep and very sexual. It was a mating of their mouths. Her mind swooned and became infused with his fever. Her fingers curled and pressed to bring his body closer, closer and impossibly closer. She moved in writhings and her gasps were uneven and breathless.

His knees spread her thighs wide and he pressed in, hard and tight. Then he moved slowly, insidiously, deliciously. He swirled inside her and rubbed his hairy belly against her smooth stomach. He taunted her breasts with his prickly chest. And his mouth was on hers, then along under her ear, and his tongue was busy tasting her.

She pressed up against him as she squirmed and moved. She curled her hips up and invited him deeper. Then she squeezed him and held him captive and dared him to try to escape.

He pulled up, then plunged back into her, joggling her. She stretched and held him yet again. She slid her knees up his flanks, and he again pulled back to swirl just inside her before he pushed in deeply to swirl again.

She wrapped her long legs around his hips and tilted to him. He began to ride her. She encouraged him, struggling, pacing, hurrying, their hearts thundering. And he took her to the brink of delight to pause there as they panted, shuddering, but he could not tarry longer, and he took her over into that wondrous dizzying freefall into the rapture of ecstasy.

They lay inert. They smiled and touched. Their breathing slowed, their heartbeats moderated and gradually they relaxed into languid movements or none at all. They sighed. His eyes were drowsy. His kisses were chaste, small pallid copies of the earlier ones.

"How much . . . was that . . . worth?"

He replied lazily, "A million dollars."

"Oh? Once more and I'm paid up for life."

His voice draggy, he demurred. "The rent's a million a day for this palatial mansion."

"Palatial?"

"You have trouble with palatial?" He appeared surprised.

"It's an unpainted box of a shack!"

He smiled and put a big rough hand on her stomach and rubbed it before sliding his hand up over her tender breasts. "It's heaven and worth every penny."

"Maybe that's what your great-grandfather thought about Lizzie."

"Lizzie could never have matched you."

"Birth control wasn't readily available in those days," she reminded him. "It was unlawful until 1936 when the Comstock law was repealed. Do you suppose Lizzie had a Mueller on the wrong side of the blanket?"

"I never heard it said."

"No rumors?"

"No."

"I wonder what hold she had on your family," Clovis mused. "She must have been awful."

"She was."

"I'm not like her."

"I know that," he said. "You're perfect."

"I think sex has blinded you. I'm not perfect."

"Really?" He curled up to lean on one elbow above her. "What are your faults?"

"Well, I can't name any right off that would involve you. But I must have some."

"The only thing I can mention is that you were rude to me at first. You were snippy and unfriendly."

"You must remember that I arrived here to find you trying to demolish my house."

"Well, yes. Which brings us to the reason a woman as young as you would be interested in being in a house this far from everything. Why did you come here?"

"I've never owned a house." She said the obvious. "I wanted to see how it would be."

"So you quit your job and hustled down."

"Oh, no. I've a whole year off. I, too, took a sabbatical."

He scoffed. "You haven't been teaching for six years."

"No, but I'm doing a book. I've done research on old folk legends concerning the flute. It is to be published."

"Well, I'll be darned."

"You thought I was here just to harass you," she guessed.

"Yeah."

"Disappointed?"

He thought about that. "Yeah. A little."

"Even if it was only harassment, you wanted to be the center of the controversy?"

"Yeah, that about covers it. And speaking of covering, brace yourself. I'll be right back."

And, naked, he went to the door, unlocked it and walked out into the hall and out of sight.

She was shocked. She got up and tiptoed so that a deaf woman couldn't hear her, and she went in search of her lover. He was in the bathroom. She waited until he came out.

He opened the door, saw her and smiled. "Couldn't wait for me, could you?"

She glanced down him. He wasn't yet satisfied and lax. Her glance fled back to his face, and he grinned. "You have your work cut out for you. I've been in a desperate condition ever since you came to this place and allowed the wind to tease your dresses and me."

"The wind?"

But that was too long to explain, so he led her back to the couch and gave her another whole different set of instructions in the care and loving of a needy Sling Mueller.

She'd read about things like that, as she tasted and fingered, licked and gnawed and rubbed, as he shifted her and maneuvered her and relished her. As they sighed and groaned and gasped, he chose different ways and experimented, but she wasn't in any hurry. She teased and distracted him, but he got the second condom.

Lying still inside her, he could feel her muscles lazily clench around him. And with her lax, he lay on his elbows, his sex still buried in her hot body, and he kissed her leisurely. He made love to her mouth and ears. She was boneless and sighing. They had all the time in the world, and the door was locked.

He toyed and touched and kneaded. He never parted from her body. And when her smooth slender arms finally slipped up around his shoulders and her mouth took his tongue to tease, he smiled and his eyes flamed.

Pressing and moving, he allowed his passion to build as slowly. With her so malleable and leisurely, their pace was at his pleasure. And he experienced all his lusty dreams with her willing body so pliant, so permissive, so obedient. "Tell me you want me," he coaxed her.

"Why do you think I'm here, naked, with my body accommodating yours, my arms around you, and my mouth just free from yours?"

He guessed. "The rent."

"You fool."

He seemed surprised. "Not the rent?"

"No."

"Why?"

She was a while replying. How could she declare herself? "I was curious. Women told me you only spoke of the ailments of cattle and horses."

"Do you want to hear about that?" He sounded somewhat surprised.

"No."

"Then why were you curious?"

She was honest. "I wanted to know what it would be like to have your attention."

"You've had that since you got out of your car that very first day."

She curled her hips. "What took you so long?"

"You're a hussy."

"Isn't that strange?" She looked up at him. "I never was until now. Do you suppose the Ghost of Lizzie Past has influenced me?"

"That coldhearted woman?"

Clovis chided. "She loved you."

"Don't be silly."

"I'll show you her letter."

"Show me you want me." He kissed along her ear.

"I already have."

"Do it again. Put your arms around me and hold me. Let me make love with you."

"I have already done that." The words became a siren's lure. "You're a greedy man."

"I was never like this before." He echoed her words. "Sex was just a real nice recreation. You make it magic. Why is that?"

"I don't know."

His voice was husky. "I like the feel of you under me."

"Me, too."

"I like the feel of you around me."

"Yes." She squeezed him.

"I like the way your breasts roil under my chest when I move this way."

"Yes."

"I can't wait any longer."

"I won't be a lot of help," she commented. "I'm frazzled."

"Are you a poor, abused, overused woman?"

"Not quite, but close."

He stopped. "Have I hurt you?"

"No, silly."

"Would it be better if I quit now?"

"No." She put her hands into his hair. "I want you to go ahead."

"Are you sure?"

"Yes."

"Oh, Clovis, you are a madness in my blood. You drive me right up the wall."

And he proved it.

Eight

It was a lazy afternoon. Sling and Clovis lay back in rocking chairs on the porch and dozed. Miss Penny came downstairs, went to the kitchen and made iced tea.

When she came out onto the porch, Sling took the tray from her and gave her his rocker. He then went around to the side porch to carry back another rocker.

They sat in peaceful silence. The two lovers had trouble not touching. Sling suggested to Clovis: "Got some stout shoes? Boots would be better. Want to walk awhile?"

"I'd love to go explore the wash," Clovis replied. "And I have some old boots." She rose from the rocker and went toward the screen door.

"Good," he said. As she went inside, he added: "Wear jeans." Then he called: "Get a hat."

She was back in a very short time. They left Miss Penny on the porch and took Spots along.

But Sling stopped at the tacky truck and buckled on his holster with its handgun. That made Clovis frown. "Why are you doing that?"

"We're very isolated out here. You never know what you might stumble across. If I should tell you to get down, you drop immediately to the ground. I'd surely hate to have to shoot through you."

"What sort of danger?"

"Not animals, not as you know them." He tilted his hat over his eyes and looked around.

"People?" She looked across to the fields and down to the thicket along the wash.

He agreed. "They're the danger."

She chided: "I thought everyone in Texas was honest, rather naive and law-abiding."

"Us natives are the minority here."

She scoffed. "White people aren't native in this land. We invaded it."

"Actually, so did all the others. But I was talking about citizens, not color. We have a lot of runners going through our lands. We have to be careful."

He took her hand, and they strolled across her lane and down toward the wash. Spots ran ahead or off to the side or trailed as his curiosity directed him.

It was very warm but not humid. Unlike the coastal cities, the Hill Country was mostly dry. In the sun, the cloth of their clothes was hot, but underneath the cloth, their skins were cooler and relatively dry. Hats were vital.

They strolled down to the wash and crossed its water-pushed rock-scrubbed bottom.

He told her, "Although it seems the ideal place, you're never to walk in a dry riverbed. The rains can be far, far away, upland. Here, the sky can be clear and the sun out. All of a sudden, you hear a strange sound and look up to see a ten-foot-high wall of water coming down the wash. We've lost a lot of Yankees that way."

So they chose a deer trail to follow. Clovis looked around the thicket of trees and brush. It was peaceful and quiet, with bird sounds. There were underbrush rustles that didn't bother Sling. She was overly alert for a while, but since he was ahead of her and watching, she began to look for the pleasure of seeing.

It was all different from Indiana.

He stopped and turned to watch her coming along the path. "You look very natural here. I think you could become acclimatized, integrated and assimilated."

"You surprise me, on occasion, with the different way you play with words. You sham."

"No. I'm not Sham, I'm Sling. After what you did with me this afternoon, you may quit calling me Mr. Mueller and you may use my first name."

"What's that?"

"Sling."

"Did your parents actually name you Sling? It's a . . . different name."

"They'd promised when I was twenty-one and mature enough, they'd tell me the story about how they named me. They would laugh and say I had to be of age to hear it. But they didn't make it that long. Who ever expects to die?"

"They didn't write the story down?"

"No. They'd told me little things here and there along the way. Not to sell off the land. To see to it the kids were educated. That sort of thing was said at odd times, just by happenstance."

"Are you curious as to why they chose Sling at all?"

"It's a good idle-time subject."

While they'd stood there talking, he'd looked beyond her and turned his head occasionally. They spoke softly. He was different again. He wasn't slouched but stood his height. His eyes seemed lazy, but his gaze was intense. And he looked at her that way.

He told her: "I can't believe you came along into my life."

"I didn't. I came down to see my cousin's legacy."

"You got more than you bargained for."

"A bear with a sore paw," she agreed.

"A lover."

She grinned. "That, especially."

"Who would ever believe such a hellcat as you were those first days, could become so friendly!"

"You were nasty." She smiled and took his big rough hand in her small smooth one.

"I can't possibly want you again."

"Uh-oh." She let go of his hand.

He pulled her to him and kissed her thoroughly. He lifted his head and looked into her eyes, then he looked aside, listening. He smiled down at her and he said, "Move up to the house."

She shook her head.

He frowned. "Are you going to be difficult?"

"Not at all. I'm just going to live in my house and play my flute and write the legends."

"You haven't mentioned making love to me." He held her head against his chest and she could hear his heart's quickening beat.

She lifted her head back to look up at him earnestly. "I thought you were all used up."

"Not entirely." He grinned. "I could probably roll you around another time or two."

She looked down at the path. "Too narrow."

"You'd just fit and you'd make it very comfortable for me."

"How like a man to think only of his own comfort."

"You'd be distracted enough," he promised.

And she laughed.

He listened and moved his head as he checked out the area.

"Is it really dangerous?"

"Not mostly." He assured her. "Want to go up on the ridge? You can see a long way from there."

"What?"

"Hills, the thicket line, the land."

"Where does this path go?"

"Thataway." The sun lines around his eyes crinkled.

"And where does it go that way?"

"Over yonder." He licked his lips to hide his smile.

"Good. That's clear. Which way are we going?"

"I'm going to get you lost so's you'll have to stay out in the brush all night with me and ruin your reputation."

"Oh?"

"Then I'll have my wily way with you and be content."

"What about me?"

"You'll enjoy every nuance."

" 'Nuance.' Yes, cowboy."

He put his fingers in his mouth and blew a shrill blast into the silence.

"Why'd you do that? Is that the bird's territorial singing?"

"Listen."

At first she heard nothing. Then she heard a slight sound that became galloping hoofbeats, and pretty soon Tucker came around the bend toward them. She laughed.

Sling petted the horse, speaking to him, his tone of voice bragging on him. But Sling was actually saying really insulting things about the time it had taken for the horse to show up. And he gave Tucker a sugar cube.

"You carry sugar with you all the time?"

"Yeah. Tucker expects it."

Tucker wasn't saddled. Sling levered himself up onto the horse's back, sat astride and reached for Clovis. He took her arm to swing her up behind him. It was more difficult, since he couldn't brace his feet in stirrups. So it took several tries before he could explain how to help him. For Clovis, it was odd to be that high, and she put her arms around Sling with her cheek against his hot back.

Sling controlled the horse with his knees. They rode along the narrow animal trails for some time. It was marvelous. They were alone in all the world.

Tucker found it interesting. He snorted once or twice. He stopped, pricked up his ears and looked off to the side, catching Sling's attention. "Coyote," Sling explained a couple of times. Once it was "Skunk." But nothing really disturbed them.

They saw a fox that ignored them but watched Spots pass him by, and they saw an armadillo. It was as if they were far into the country...and Clovis realized that actually they were just so, even at the house.

Along the brush by the wash was different. It felt very isolated. At the house, there was the link to civilization. Out in the brush, the link wasn't there.

Anything could happen. Who would find them? The buzzards. Yes. The circling buzzards would call attention to them. In that countryside, circling buzzards were always checked out to find what had attracted the scavengers' attention.

Somewhere in that maze, Sling stopped Tucker and slid off the horse. He reached up for Clovis. As the two lovers stood together, Sling slapped the horse's back end and said, "Home."

And the horse trotted off.

"How does he know where it is?"

"This is where we picked him up. The barn is just over the hill on the other side of the thicket."

Clovis looked around. The brush didn't look any different there than it had everywhere else along the way. As Sling led the way, supposedly back to her house, Clovis asked, "Do you leave Tucker out of the corral?"

"No. When I whistled, he jumped the fence."

"Oh. Then he comes and goes as he chooses?"

Sling was sure. "Not without a whistle."

"How did you train him that way?"

He grinned. "Sugar."

"You're going to rot his teeth."

"He brushes twice a day," Sling assured her.

And she laughed.

They came to a place where the wash ran into a culvert under a gravel road. "I don't remember this."

"It's your road."

"Ahhh. But we can't go any farther. I'm dying of thirst."

"Well, then, we'll go back."

He led her back into the thicket, and she heard a car. "Someone is on the road."

"Yes."

"Oh, did you see the car?"

"Yes." His word was short.

"Who was it?"

"Greg. Your lawyer."

"Oh," she said again. Then she mentioned: "He tried to dance with me last night."

"I know."

"Aren't you going to allow me to see my lawyer?"

"No."

She said logically, "I can go to his office."

"You can see him then. I'll go along."

"Why?"

"You want me to say it?" He stopped and turned to face her.

She looked up and smiled just a little. "I think so."

"I don't want some fool trying for you while I have my mark on you. You're off-limits to him and any other male for this time. Those are the facts." He was sober faced and watching her.

"And . . . I have nothing to say in the matter?"

"No." He waited. Then he leaned his head forward just a bit. "Do you object?"

"Not so far."

"You do have to understand, Clovis, that I'm not a marrying man. But I've never had this problem before. You're like an itch inside me. I crave you. I need you like Tucker needs the sugar." He moved slowly, took her into his arms and held her to him. "God, woman, you are driving me crazy. I've never had this want for any other woman. I don't like you out of my sight. Then I see you, and I don't want you away from arm's reach. And I hold you and I want you. I haven't had a good night's sleep since I first saw you."

"Why aren't you a marrying man?"

"I've done all the work part of that for the last fifteen years. Since I was nineteen and my folks died, I've had the six kids on my neck. The kids, along with the ranch, those three old ladies at home and Lizzie like a buzzard sitting over here, ready to pick my bones. I don't want to go through that again."

"I see."

"What's that mean?"

She tilted her head back to look up into his face. "I understand."

"And you're willing for us to just go along together?"

"I'll see."

"Now, what's *that* mean?"

"I believe I'd like to marry. So I should guard my reputation, and my conduct should be circumspect."

"You trying to blackmail me into marrying you?"

"Not at all." She patted his cheek and released herself from his embrace. "You want your life one way, and I want mine another. We are not suited."

"Hell! I was honest with you, and now you're going to give me a hard time."

"A hard time?"

"You're going to shut me out."

"Oh, I don't *think* so. At least not right away. I like the way we have sex."

"I made love to you."

"No." She looked around as if the conversation bored her. "We enjoyed each other's bodies."

"Now, Clovis—"

She smiled at him and said, "Since Greg's gone, we can go back. Which trail do I take?" She studied the ground and the trails with interest. "Wait. Let me guess. I just get up onto the road and go over to the lane. Right?" She started across the wash to a path that led up to the road.

"Clovis. Don't go off that way. We have to talk."

She turned back and looked at him in surprise. "We did. You said I am wearing your temporary mark. And I said that was okay for now."

"Clovis..." But what she'd said was true. Why was he so irritated by her simple summation of their exchange? Scowling, he followed her until they got onto the road, then he walked beside her. Spots ran ahead. It wasn't far. They turned into the lane, and she covered a yawn.

Then she stretched discreetly.

He watched her.

She flashed a smile up at him and said, "I believe I'll nap. Would you like a piece of the cake before you leave?"

She was telling him to run along.

She said, "I really loved seeing the thicket. I would never have had the nerve to go in by myself. Thank you."

"You're welcome. Clovis—"

But she was signaling to Miss Penny. "Sling needs a piece of your cake." She indicated Sling, mimed eating and wrote *cake* on her hand. Then she pointed to herself, yawned, patting her mouth, then put her hands up by her cheek and closed her eyes.

She smiled sweetly at Sling and said, "I really enjoyed the walk. Thanks again."

"Clovis—"

"I'll be in touch."

Now, because he had used it himself, he knew that was the greatest put-off in this modern world. And he was shaken by his reaction.

Numb, he followed Miss Penny into the kitchen because he wasn't functioning well enough to just leave. He had a glass of water, forgot the cake, patted Miss Penny's shoulder and left.

Neither woman was there the next morning. Spots was glad to see him. They wandered around the porches. The doors were locked, there was no note, and Sling was very frustrated.

They weren't back at suppertime. He called about ten. With the light blinking on the phone, it was Miss Penny who lifted the receiver and said, "Please call tomorrow."

How could he talk to a deaf woman? Sling was defeated. He went up to the attic and looked over at her house. The lights were on, and he could see the shadow of Miss Penny on the curtain. Could Greg sit out on the lane and see Clovis's shadow on her curtain? And for the first time in his life, Sling knew jealousy.

He got over there very early the next morning and sat on their porch. They came out in a bustle, dressed for the city. They both greeted him with apparent cordial delight and apologized for leaving . . . as they left.

What the hell was that woman up to? Was she trying to irritate him? Or was she trying to ease him off?

Again, the two didn't return until late. Sling got there after supper, sat on the porch and waited for them.

Even the car was slow and hesitated when the headlights came to his tacky pickup. Then they drove up next to it and Clovis got out slowly. "Where are you?" Clovis called.

He stood up.

"It *is* you?"

And he realized Spots hadn't run to greet them, and they hadn't been sure who was there.

"Sling," Sling told her. "Spots's up here with me."

"I don't know this truck very well. Did you have to junk the other one?"

Sling relaxed a little. She was treating him in a normal way. "Naw. They're fixing it. The windshield's a mess."

"We were lucky." She was holding Miss Penny's arm and walking slowly. "I don't believe you ever told me if the people were pleased to get the meat."

"Very. And they'll make moccasins from the hide."

"Good."

"Summer skins are pretty light. Have you been avoiding me?" That question popped out and surprised even him.

"Why, of course not. Why would you say that?"

"Because you've not seen me in two whole days."

"Oh. Was there something wrong?"

"Yes!" He snapped the word. "I haven't seen you."

She stood in the starlight. "Headache?"

"You need a good swat."

She lifted her chin. "Oh, no. I do not."

"I just said you needed one. I wasn't threatening you."

He'd come down the steps and was helping Miss Penny up them. He asked Clovis tersely, "Where have you been?"

"Shopping."

"For two days?"

"Miss Penny can't rush from one store to another."

"What did she need? I'll pay."

"Oh, didn't I mention it? I'm giving her a fee for chaperoning me, and she is making quite good money with her mending."

"I still don't have my shirt and pants back."

"We hadn't known you were in that big of a hurry. We'll get them to you day after tomorrow. Will that be all right?"

"Send Miss Penny to bed. I want to talk to you."

"Is it something urgent? I'm really bushed."

"Yes."

"Well, just a minute. I'll be right out."

She took Miss Penny into the house and went up the stairs with her. It was some time before she came back down. She was still dressed for the city. She hadn't changed into wearing only a soft, easily removable robe. She was bent on making him squirm.

He was half sitting on the banister, one forearm on a thigh, the other hand on his hip. His Stetson was hanging off the knob of a rocking chair. He was watching her come from the lighted house onto the darkened porch.

She was breathtaking.

She put her hands up to cup the sides of her eyes. "Where are you?"

"If you'd turned off the hall light, you'd be able to see."

"Oh. Of course. How is Chin? Still surviving his cooking?"

"He's a good cook."

"And Tom? Who is he chasing this week?"

"Not you?"

"I'm not his style."

"How do you know that?"

"He told me right away. He said he didn't want me to get my hopes up. Isn't it too bad that you weren't as honest?"

"I never made any promises to you."

"I know that."

"Then why are you acting this way?"

She shrugged in the dim light reflected onto the porch. And with her complete honesty, she told him, "I'm . . . disappointed."

That word hit him in his stomach and he even made a soft sound from the blow.

She walked over into the dark part of the porch and looked out over the night.

He followed, miserably, to stand beside her, and he sighed. There were billions and billions of stars up there. And they, none of them, had any idea what it was like to try to deal with a woman.

He looked down at her, and her blond hair shimmered in the scant light. She was little-boned and not at all strong, and she had him tied in knots. What was he to do about her? He said in a roughened voice, "I've missed seeing you."

"Good."

"Were you gone deliberately, just to punish me?"

"I'm not that nasty."

"I need a kiss."

"Oh. So do I." She said that as she quickly turned to him and lifted her arms to put them around his shoulders.

He snatched her to him with a terrible groan. "Damn you."

She laughed shakily.

He scrubbed his hands up and down her back, pressing her to him; then he wound his arms around her and simply held her against him.

Her breaths were broken.

"Are you laughing at me?" He snarled the words.

"No." The word was uneven.

"I ... Clovis ... I ... Damn."

"I agree wholeheartedly."

"With *what* are you agreeing?"

"With your confusion. I, too, am confused. You haven't given me the kiss you offered."

And he kissed her.

At first he wasn't kind. He ground his mouth into hers, but she whimpered. He lifted his mouth a hairsbreadth, then he kissed her as he should have all along. It was exquisite.

Finally, he lifted his head and whooshed his breath as he held her. He didn't even offer to let go of her. He kissed her again and again, coaxingly, and she responded.

Her breaths shivered and her hands pawed at him and at his clothes. He gasped, "Why, Clovis!" And he groaned, "Are you sure?" And he said, "My love—"

She said, "Once more, for old times' sake."

That stopped him cold. "What are you saying?"

"I want you one more time."

"One?"

She nodded little jerks as she began to peel him out of his clothes.

He was dismayed, but he wasn't sure he could resist her. They really needed to sort this out. She was trying to put him back in the herd. He didn't want that. He said, "Just a minute." Then he went to his pickup, ostensibly to fetch some protection for her, but actually to give them a break from the lightning streak of need that flickered between them.

He came back to her, ready to talk first, but she was naked. She was standing there, waiting for him, and as he approached, she lifted her arms up and moved her feet a step apart.

He was lost.

They scrabbled him out of his clothing. Yet, as feverish as they were, they relished each movement, each touch, each feeling, as they made love to each other. It was something. No one ever really believed such ecstasy actually happened in real life.

The lovers took a long, delaying time about it. And their pantings of desire were thrilling to each other. The touches were exquisitely sensual, and they were lifted to rapture as they mated and parted and teased. They became so sensitized that each little touch or flick of a finger or swirl of a tongue made them shudder and shiver there on the crumbling brink of delight.

Their eyes were wet with their emotions. Their moans were hushed and smothered by kisses. Their greedy hands slipped on bodies dewed by sexual heat. And their hunger was awesome.

They were so needy and that need so concentrated, that their couplings were thrilling excitements to every nerve in their entire bodies. He would touch her here and her chest would rise to his lips. He would touch her there and her hips would tilt in pleas.

He moved over her like a feeding beast, tasting her. And she writhed in her need of him, opening to him, begging.

She would push him back and climb onto him, frantic, and he would lie, his hot eyes intent as he controlled her.

She would release him and give him the same treatment. Teasing, tempting, touching, denying. She pushed him too far and he took control, taking her and moving slowly, slowly, before he allowed her to set her pace and carry them both to paradise.

She became aware for the first time that they were on the bare boards of the porch. "How rude of you to take me on the floor. I have splinters from one end to the other. I thought gentlemen always made the ladies a soft bed."

"You jumped me before I could get us inside."

"I jumped you? I don't remember that. I came out to say good-night and that's the last coherent thought I can recall. What happened to me?"

"I did."

"You sound very masculinely smug."

"I am replete." His words dragged.

"Is it catching?"

His words were slowed. "I just gave you a sustaining dose of it."

"So that's what it's called. I thought it was just called 'sex.'"

"Clovis, we need to talk."

"Not now. I can't gather my brain cells toward organized thought."

"I believe I like you best with your thoughts disorganized."

"I can probably play my flute now, better than ever. I will let the flute play instead of trying to control it."

"Ahhh."

"Come up on the roof."

And naked in the warm summer night, like Pan and one of the sylphs who haunted the air, they did go there. She played like one who yearned. Her music was beautiful. It touched in his soul as he lay back on one of the chairs. He was gloriously naked. All that he needed was a crown of flowers.

And Clovis?

She played from her heart. She wove her music around the man who lay back listening to her. And she cast a spell on him.

Nine

They went down to the living room where they had dropped their clothing, but they didn't dress. Clovis opened a drawer of a Mueller-branded old desk and gave Sling a sheaf of papers.

He glanced at her, puzzled. "These your papers?"

"Yes."

He scanned several and frowned. "These are the originals. Why doesn't your lawyer have them in his safe?"

She smiled and curled down on the Victorian fainting couch to watch him.

Naked, he leaned back on a needlepoint armless rocker. The hair pattern of his body, arms and legs was well-done. He looked like the living statue of a Roman warrior, home from battle. One knee was bent and that foot was planted squarely on the floor. His other leg was stretched out, lax, resting on the heel, the foot leaning to the side. He was beautiful.

He set the papers on the round, marble-topped table next to the chair, and unfolded the letter on top of the modest stack. He read aloud:

> "To: Clovis Culpepper
>   Music Department
>   Indiana University
>   Bloomington, Indiana

> "Dear Miss Culpepper,
> "From my long search, you are my only surviving relative. There is actually no kinship at all, but you are the only one I can claim."

Sling glanced up at Clovis. "I'll bet that shivered you in your boots. You thought she was begging, didn't you?"

Clovis barely shook her head. Her eyes were soft and mysterious.

> "You are my heiress. I have lived in this house for sixty-seven years, and it is mine. I have papers that will help you in your claim. They will be in the second drawer, lower right-hand side of the desk in the living room.
> "This land now belongs to Sling Mueller. He may resist your claim.
> "I know that you are unmarried. You should look him over. He's a good man."

Sling glanced over at Clovis. Nude, she was curled

on her side with her knees drawn up partway. Her lower arm was bent up over her breasts with that hand on her opposite shoulder. Her other arm was lax and that hand was curled off the edge of the sofa. She was asleep.

His hand holding the letter slowly sank to the edge of the chair by his hip, and he simply looked at her. Her hair was a halo of pale gold in the lamp's light. Her skin was so delicate. Her bones were fragile. She was so feminine.

His sex stirred. But his eyes saw the grace of her female body. The curves and dips of her shoulder, waist and hip, the way her thigh rounded and narrowed so perfectly to the knee and on to her slender ankle and precious foot. She was a miracle.

He studied the grace of her wrist so defenselessly curled off the edge of the sofa. And he lifted his own hand to study its rough, square bluntness. As he clenched his fist, he compared the male power to the delicate miracle of her hand.

The sight of her eyelashes touched oddly in his heart. Her smooth brows were a poor comparison to the bushy tangle of his. And her lips were...rose petals.

He had never looked on a woman as he now viewed Clovis. His face was gentle, his body lax, his sex stirring. But he didn't move to her. He curled forward to touch her hand, then stopped. She was sleeping so soundly.

He put the letter aside, then leaned back on the chair, crossed his arms on his chest, disregarded his need for her and simply watched her sleep. His love.

And he knew then that he was beginning to love her.

After a long while, he rose, went up the stairs to her room and turned down her bedcovers. Then he went back for her, carrying her gently, her body cool against the heat of his, her arms sleepily creeping up around his shoulders.

He put her into her bed, covering her carefully. He stood up, ignored his need and looked down on her. She was his.

He went downstairs, gathered his clothing and put it on. He took hers back upstairs. He turned off lights, locked the front door and told Spots to guard. He stood on the porch, not wanting to leave. Knowing that for her sake he could not stay, he went down the steps to his tacky pickup and went home.

The next morning, Sling took a crew over and put up the chicken fence that he'd opposed. Clovis was delighted. The crew never did recover from their astonishment. Tom bit his lip the entire time to keep from laughing. He just nodded or shook his head, his Stetson covering the humor spilling from his eyes.

The men did a good job. They shot looks at Sling and thereby got his silent permission to do everything her way. She was boss. And she was picky.

They had to put a special rim of perforated metal along the bottom of the chicken wire. The metal had to extend below the tightly packed ground level so that nothing could dig under the wire.

And Clovis had to have a bale of hay. That was easily done. Tom went over to the Mueller barn and brought back four. She needed only one. She asked the cost. They were all astonished. Sling charged her an apple pie. Miss Penny made several. The men had the pies for dessert after Clovis fed them a hearty lunch.

The fence enclosure was round. There was a gate. The gate gave them the most trouble. But it was finally made to her satisfaction. And it was worth all the effort just to see her smile. She clasped her hands and looked around in pure delight.

Then she asked how did one make a nest?

Ranch hands never really want to admit to farming. But Peter was old enough not to mind the teasing and he showed Clovis how to do that. And it was he who constructed the nest shelves inside that ratty, old, preservative-painted chicken shack.

Peter even made a couple of slanted access ramps to make it easier for the chickens to get up to the elevated house. The ramps were fixed so that the boards were too high for egg-stealing snakes.

So in town—just that quick—Sling heard inventive variations of: "Hear you're starting a chicken ranch?"

Sling was patient.

He was bent on seeing to it that Clovis got so involved in the community that she couldn't leave.

He went to the bank and saw the new president, who was Randolph Tylor. Sling went to Randy's office and Randy said, "Well, Sling! Howdy. Come in and sit yourself down. I hear tell you're going into the chicken business." And he laughed: "Har, har, har."

"Not quite." Sling smiled. Then he said, "Miss Culpepper showed me the papers she has that Lizzie gave her. There are some indications that Lizzie paid the taxes on the place until my parents died. Do you have any record of her income?"

"Well, Sling, that's been something confidential, handed down from one head to the next—twice now in these years. She had an income." He steepled his fingers and looked important and knowing.

"There are some clues that it came from our Trust. Is that right?"

"Well. We never mention where it came from."

"How much was it?"

"It was started long ago. Back when a man could live easy making a hundred a month. She got three hundred. That never changed."

"No cost-of-living increases?"

"Such wasn't known in those days. He—the board thought she'd be comfortable the rest of her life."

"Who?"

"I'm not at liberty to tell."

"I want the income to be given to Miss Culpepper just as if it is a part of Lizzie's legacy."

"Well, now. There was no will. I don't believe— We did have a letter saying to turn over Lizzie's account here to Miss Culpepper. We've notified her of that, but of course, there is a year's waiting period in case there might be any outstanding debts."

"I want the three hundred paid to Miss Culpepper each month, beginning now."

"Why don't you wait until after she sues?"

"It's my Trust. I ask it to be done now."

"This would be highly irregular. You must realize that. If she knows anything about the law, or if Greg hears of this, he'll...wonder. Are you sure that you want Miss Culpepper to be given three hundred dollars a month for the rest of her life?"

"As her legacy from her cousin."

"Well, now, I... Well, it *is* your money."

"Yes. See to it for me, will you, Randy?"

"In confidence? Just like for Lizzie?"

"Please."

"I'll see to it. We appreciate your business. Your Trust is one of our mainstays, you know that."

"I appreciate all the care and consideration you've given the family."

"Yes, sir. Thank you. I'll see to this right away."

So in another day or so, when the chickens were delivered and they were fluttering around in the circular enclosure, Sling came with some of his crew to help. He took that opportunity to say to a distracted, delighted Clovis, "I believe you actually do have a legitimate claim on this land."

"You josh."

"No. And I've decided to ask you to marry me."

She looked at him soberly in the midst of all that flurry of chicken debate, and she said, "You choose an odd time for a proposal. Such timing would make it appear that you have been driven to it. You know you're not the marrying kind."

"A man does as he must." He smiled his best killer smile at her to melt her into her boot tops.

Unmelted, she said, "So you'd sacrifice yourself to protect the borders of your land?"

"I'd get fringe benefits."

"You don't want to be married. You can't have changed your mind this soon."

"I want you." That was too intense, so he moved a little and gestured with one hand. "Your claim is good. You would win a suit."

And she laughed. "Of course not."

"Not? You hired Greg—"

"That was only to annoy you. I have no claim on this land at all. But when I drove up and saw you trying to pull down this house, it really ticked me. I overreacted. I knew which of those men was you. I impulsively wanted to thwart you. I was only down here to see this 'cousin' whom I didn't know had just been buried. I was curious to see what sort of house this was, and incidentally, to do as Lizzie suggested— to take a look at you."

Sling watched her. "How did I do?"

"We don't suit. You're not interested in marriage. I am."

"Well. I just asked you. Should I have gotten down on my knees?"

"You don't mean it. I'll stay the year, if you don't mind. I love it here. I'll get my book done and go back to Indiana. Then you can pull down the house, if you can."

She'd stay a year? So he had some time to convince her. But . . . if she really didn't have any hope of getting the land, why had she put up the elaborate pole-and-board shade over the house? Why was she spending her money on the chickens? He frowned at her. Maybe she just needed coaxing.

He sighed deeply, shifted his stance, spread his hands on his hips and looked over the chickens, then out over the peaceful land. And he wondered what she'd do next. Maybe she was just trying for his attention? He'd give it to her. He said, "When's your party for the people around here? To let them see that roof and the shade structure you set up. You owe a social engagement to about everybody around, by now."

"I thought next week. I'd put a notice in the area paper and the church bulletin. Is it possible anyone would be missed, that way?"

"No. But don't put it in the paper. You could get some strange attention. Of course, you could have just told Natalie Comstock. We're spread so thin that any news is interesting. Everybody already knows about the chickens, and Natalie wasn't even the first to hear it."

Then he cast a glance at her. "You are including my people, aren't you? They were very willing to put up that chicken fence. For ranch hands to do that, was really a favor to you."

"Of course, they're invited. I'll never forget how kind they were to Miss Penny at your place."

"Come again this Sunday?"

"Why, thank you, landlord."

"And Miss Penny."

"Thank you."

"I'm courting you."

"Oh. I just thought you were being neighborly. This puts a different slant on the invitation."

"I'm making sure everyone knows I mean to trap you."

"It must be the challenge." She shook her head. "You know I'm leery of your offer. You can't love me. You're only interested in keeping the land."

"The land is important, no question. Do you know that Milo Fuquey is seriously thinking of dividing his land into two-acre plots and selling them to Yankee retirees as 'ranchettes'?"

"No."

"Yes.

"Why just Yankees?"

"They'll pay more. Milo will make a bundle. The Yankees didn't beat Texas during The War Between the States, so they're coming down here, now, and buying it in pieces. It won't be no time at all till they own us, lock, stock and barrel."

"Are you going to split up your land into 'ranchettes'?"

"No."

"What will you do?"

"I don't know. Water is a problem. Right now, New Mexico is trying to pay penalties for the water not delivered to Texas by the Pecos River. We don't want the money, we want the water. Think of that. Already, water is more important than money. You can't drink money."

She looked off over the land. "Just to look, it seems so simple. There's all this land. Living down here is really very complicated. But it is up north, too. We have rivers in Indiana so polluted that the fish can't be eaten."

"We've never allowed any wastes to be buried on our land," he told her. "The scary thing is that the government wants to bury really hazardous wastes out here. Del Rio has been on their ears about it. It's a constant struggle. A constant vigilance. We all have to pay attention. If we don't, we turn around and the damage is done. Then we have to try to undo it."

She watched him soberly. "I hope you win."

"I hope we survive."

"You will."

He lowered his eyes so that she wouldn't see how earnest he was. "I'll need your help."

She laughed.

"Now, how can you react that way to the survival of this land?"

"You're really stacking it up." She shook her head chidingly.

"No," he denied it. "I need you to give me heart. Without you, I might not care."

"As strongly as your people have defended this land in these several hundred years, you'd do it all by yourself."

He ventured: "I have the hunch that you're resisting me."

"No," she demurred. "I'm protecting myself. My preservation."

"If you give me hope, I'll preserve you, too."

"The threat to me—" her voice was strangely quiet "—is you."

He protested: "How can you believe that?"

She saw that he was truly dismayed. She frowned a little, puzzled.

Two roosters went at each other and that distracted only Clovis. She yelled, "Stop them!"

Annoyed, Sling turned to see what was happening, and saw that the men were laughing. No trouble there. It was the roosters? She was worried about the roosters? He said, "They'll figure it out."

Indignantly, she retorted: "I've heard about rooster fights!"

"Honey, those two roosters are just schoolboys seeing who'll back off. They aren't wearing metal spurs. Leave them alone."

The din was incredible. The hens were all squawking. The men were cheering and giving advice . . . and betting. And the dog ran around the outside of the fence and barked.

Clovis ran over, got the hose, turned it on and "accidentally" lost control of the bucking hose and flicked water over everybody—men and chickens. The squawking then was really something. And the doused roosters ran out of reach; then, poised rather bedraggled, walked stiffly in indignation.

Clovis hadn't been so stupid as to hit Sling with the water, but he stood there with his hands on his hips and a very patient look. "You're interfering with the pecking order."

"Males are totally beyond comprehension."

He was reasonable. "Even cows have a form of pecking order. It's the way of the world."

"And you're on the top of the heap." She lifted her chin and dared him to discipline her in front of all those fascinated listeners.

Sling slowly took off his hat to hold it courteously between his hands. He said levelly, "Yes, ma'am."

It was brilliantly done.

The men stood silently. Sling hadn't given an inch, but he hadn't brought her down, either. She considered him. There was more to Sling than she'd realized. That made her thoughtful.

She and Miss Penny again fed the men a lunch of great sandwiches in all sorts of combinations. There were also French fries, fruits and the usual strong coffee. Added to that were two cakes. The men ate every crumb. They said it was nice not to have to eat Chin's food—and worry. Then they laughed real dirty.

After lunch, the Mueller crew went home. Sling stayed. He made jobs for himself around the chicken fence as he taught Spots that the chickens weren't there to entertain him. From the porch, Clovis watched that. Sling was gentle and patient with the dog.

Only occasional differences disturbed those new occupants confined within the fenced area, and the rest of the day was peaceful.

On the back porch, near the kitchen door, was a new drum of chicken feed. When evening came, Miss Penny took an apron off the hook behind the cupboard door and carefully tied it on. She went to the drum and lifted the lid, gathered the bottom of the apron up and put a scoop of feed into the fold. Then, smiling and holding on to the stair rail, she went carefully down the steps and out to the chickens.

Since the roosters weren't yet settled, Sling suggested that Miss Penny throw the feed through the fence. She walked along, doing that.

Clovis came to stand beside Sling. "Now you know why I got the chickens."

He put his hand around the nape of her neck and said, "I love you."

"You know you're not the marrying kind."

"How do you know that?"

"You told me so."

"But I proposed to you."

"That was a fluke. You like rolling me around on the splinters of the porch."

He watched her.

"I was misled by Lizzie's admonition to look you over. I thought she'd checked you out."

"You think you know me?"

"Yes. It's by genes from Eve."

"I really do love you. You slept last night while I watched you. I wanted you, but I left you alone. That should prove something."

"I really thought you only were attracted to older women."

"And you. Let me back."

Such odd words. But with them, she knew he did understand that she was hesitant to give him her full trust again.

He asked, "What will it take?"

"I'm not sure."

He rubbed his nose thoughtfully. "I could get you pregnant. That might clue you in to my commitment to you."

"Yeah. Or you'd panic and take off." Then she looked up into his face and said, "Or I would read regret in your eyes every time I looked at you."

He groaned and pulled her head to his chest. "I'll find a way."

The next day, the two women again went to town. Spots was left with the responsibility of the chickens. A very occupied dog.

Sling stayed for supper. Miss Penny was amused. "I thought I was here to chaperon Miss Culpepper. Why are you here, too?"

He pointed to his chest, circled his eyes with his thumbs and forefingers, then pointed to Miss Penny. He watched her.

She thought that was hilarious.

Sling told Clovis, "Too bad she can't hear. She's a humorous, cheerful woman. Not like Lizzie."

"You've almost convinced me that Lizzie was a pain in the neck."

"She was that. But she might have been lonely out here."

"You tried three women as her companions."

"Maybe what she really wanted was a man." He slid salacious eyes over to her.

"If Miss Penny could hear, you'd probably not be able to think of anything decent enough for her ears."

"I know how to talk to old ladies, and I can play a really mean hand of bridge. I got so good and was so heartless about it, that they wouldn't let me play with them." He smiled.

"You are devious."

"I'm a winner. If I want to do something, I do it the best I know how, and I win. I let you slip back, but I'll do my damnedest to get you. All's fair... Don't forget that."

Miss Penny continued serenely, daintily eating her supper.

And afterward, in the late-fading light of evening, the three went out to inspect the chicken yard. The chickens were huddled in groups. Some were venturing into the strange house and staking claims. They were "talking," making sounds. The roosters were dry, their feathers were magnificent, so they were strutting and eyeing each other.

The three humans stood there, and the two women were satisfied. Sling warned Spots again. And the long, skinny tailed, short-haired, liver-spotted dog smiled. He was in control.

So it was the next morning that Sling arrived on the porch. And again the ladies were gone. But there was a paper on the door. He got out of his newly repaired, magnificent pickup and looked around. The chickens were settling in.

Spots came to greet Sling. The man squatted down and rubbed the dog. "I miss you. You know that? But you're doing a great job here. I appreciate it."

The dog laughed and danced with his front feet in place and whipped the air with his long, skinny tail.

The note said: "We'll be back about two this afternoon."

Sling returned at that specified time and was sitting on the porch, waiting, when they drove up. He stood and watched them exit the car. He called, "No packages?"

"No." And the women looked at each other and laughed.

"Just what have you two been up to that you're acting so sly?"

And Miss Penny replied, "You're very nosy."

"I've never deni—" And Sling's face went blank. Then his smile dawned slowly and in delight. "You can *hear!* You can!" And he jumped down the steps and went to her. "Can you really, you rascally woman?"

"Yep!" Her face was a wreath of smiles. All her wrinkles were patterned into delight.

Sling glanced over at Clovis, who was wet eyed and smiling, and his love for her hurt his chest.

"Well," Sling said with a big grin. "I *suppose* I'll have to try to clean up my language if a lady is going to be listening."

And that snippy old lady said, "I read lips quite well."

His face fell. "Then you can't hear me?"

She put a hand on his arm and said gently, "Yes. They fixed me. I have two hearing aids, and they cleaned out a lot of wax. It was mostly wax. And I can hear the *chickens* talking! Listen!" She turned from Sling and began to walk over to the chicken yard, putting her hand on Spots's head as she went along.

Sling turned back to Clovis. Her smile was still so tender, and the happy tears had spilled over. So did his heart. "My God, woman. I love you."

"You were really glad for her."

"Yes."

"Oh, Sling..."

Ten

For people involved with animals and the land, the weekends had to be preserved for social intercourse. Even then, with the chancy weather and ailing livestock, not all the people could make it to a gathering.

But being as dispersed as they were in that area, they did make the social effort. People too long alone can get peculiar, set in their ways and difficult for other people.

"How many will come?" Clovis asked Ethel Lambert as they had iced tea on the Lambert porch.

"All of them. They are more curious about Sling's conduct than they are about the shade you've contrived. That was enormously clever. Jaff said he wished he'd thought of it first."

"Why is he limping?"

"Well, you know by now that on occasion he still rides something that doesn't want to be ridden. This last animal was particularly opposed."

"Oh."

"Natalie and I are bringing either salads or cakes. Which would you prefer we bring?"

"Oh, that's very kind of you, but Miss Penny and I can manage."

Ethel inquired, "How many are you anticipating?"

"Fifty?"

Ethel shook her head. "At least twice that."

"Uh-oh."

"Yes. Let the rest of us bring something. The others will start offering this week. That's so you don't buy too much or run short. We're used to this. We've done it so much that we can just about judge who'll show up and who won't, according to the occasion. You do realize those who are musically inclined will bring their instruments? They'll bring their own chairs. Have your flute handy."

"I'll look forward to that part."

Then Ethel smiled at Clovis. "Fredricka is very fond of you. She is so pleased you've decided to stay for this year. I am curious about your book. Have you begun?"

"I began collecting the legends several years ago. I have to organize the material and get it written. This will be a small book, with a rather limited appeal."

"I'd be curious to read it. I make a good proofreader."

"I'll bring some pages by," Clovis promised.

"Good. And accept the offers of help for your gathering. It makes people feel involved."

"Thank you for your advice." Clovis smiled. "I'll do that."

"Miss Penny was lucky to land on you."

"You have to know that Sling was being asinine when he brought her there."

"Territorial," Ethel agreed.

"Yes. He was afraid I'd get a toehold on his land."

Ethel blinked, then laughed.

Clovis thought Texans were a little strange. They laughed at odd times.

In the next week, Miss Penny took some pleasure in answering the phone and taking messages. The offers of food poured in. Miss Penny kept track of that. Fredricka and several of the other younger women volunteered to help serve the food. It appeared that there would be more than a hundred people.

Clovis asked Sling, "How am I going to get all those people into the house and up on the roof so that they can see the shade?"

"We'll run them through a few at a time."

"But how will they all eat at once?"

"The boys will help set up tables in the yard."

Clovis looked at the weed lot that was her yard and said, "Oh."

So she shouldn't have been surprised when some of the "boys" came over from the Mueller place and mowed the weeds. With the weeds controlled, the house looked only eccentric. Without the pole-and-board shade contraption, the house would have looked tacky.

But the surprise was that they mowed the rise over between her house and the Muellers' place, as well. How many people could be coming? And Clovis was unsettled.

Ethel sent her cleaning crew over to tidy the house and wax the furniture. Natalie sent flowers already in vases that were a little odd but in that house, they looked right at home.

On Thursday, Sling and a couple of his men delivered a great commercial ice chest and hooked it up on the back porch by the kitchen door. It was a godsend in that heat. The weather was turning muggy.

On Friday, a tropical storm in the Caribbean was on its way north, but it was probably heading toward the panhandle of Florida. That was far enough away, but everyone around said they just hoped to God they'd get some of it here, inland, in the Hill Country. Clovis said, "After lunch."

And the musicians said, "After we play."

Most of the food was delivered on Saturday and almost all of it was put into the great ice chest. That night the weather report was that the storm would probably veer west of Alabama on to Mississippi and maybe a little bit over into Louisiana. Texas could get some "moisture" north of Houston. That meant it would miss the Hill Country. And those people who came by groaned about always missing any rain. Clovis again said, "After lunch."

Some of the more delicate things were brought over early on Sunday. And almost all were particular about where their culinary contributions were stored and how they'd be served. "It didn't turn out the way it should." That was almost de rigueur for those greatly practiced cooks to disparage their perfectly done dishes. Shameless bids for praise.

Clovis was almost too distracted, but Miss Penny was practiced in responses. She stroked the egos.

Sling and his crew set up the borrowed sawhorses and board tables in the mowed-weed yard.

As Sunday progressed, skies were lowering. An anxious check with the weather station said the storm might be more in Louisiana than in Mississippi. It was moving slowly, and they didn't expect landfall until late. Unless that front coming in from the north would weaken and the heat of the water would make the up-draft stronger, then the storm just might push farther west.

Miss Penny and Clovis went to church eyeing the skies. Clovis was anxious, but Miss Penny said serenely, "It'll be all right."

Then Sling met them at the church door. He'd gotten there early so he could do exactly that; and to Clovis's frustration, he sat with them. It was as if they'd planned it that way. He was, indeed, very territorial. And Clovis's cheeks were charmingly flushed with her feelings of self-consciousness, while her body was only aware of his next to hers.

But Clovis gradually became aware that Miss Penny was able to *listen* to the preacher. She glanced to see Miss Penny's contentment, and her heart was touched.

After the service, everyone went to the Shade house. And the fact that it was Sling's but claimed by Clovis—and they'd been sitting together in church— lent a delicious titillation to the affair.

Sling then organized everyone. People walked around outside to inspect the shade; and in groups, they trooped up the stairs to the roof. There, some leaned over the railing, looked around and called down to people below on the porch or out in the mowed yard.

There were the usual number of children with more-than-average curiosity and adventurousness. The chickens were run around by children waving arms and hollering on the other side of the fence. Several adults chided, "Now, now."

Clovis was indignant, so Sling slouched over and said softly, "Cut it out or I'll thrash you."

One kid ran to his mother saying, "Sling said he'd thrash me!"

And the kid's father said, "Good idea."

The mother was appalled and hugged the child and scolded the father.

Then Tom sassed a young woman and patted her fanny, and another woman became upset.

And Sling told Clovis's lawyer, Greg, "You have really beautiful teeth."

Greg smiled widely, showing them off.

But Sling said, "If you don't ignore Miss Culpepper, I'm going to smash them."

Greg's smile faded.

So everything wasn't exactly peaches and cream. But all in all, it was a lighthearted time under that threatening sky, and Clovis was impressed by how practiced those her own age were in organizing and feeding that number of people. The contrived tables had been covered with paper, but most of the women had brought tablecloths and more flowers. Everyone brought their own chairs.

There was thunder! And people exclaimed, "Did you hear that?" And they asked in a practiced manner, "What was that?" and they said, "Hey, you kids, that's *thunder!*" They were all unabashed hambones, so there were groans.

But the rain held off. And after the visitors had devastated all the platters and bowls of perfectly concocted foods, they tidied up, folded the cloths and put the flowers together in a tub on the porch. The mass of colors was very pretty against the weathered wood of the house.

Then they took their chairs and walked in a stream over to the slope that divided Clovis's place from Sling's. There, under the wide and threatening sky, they seated themselves up along the gentle slope while the musicians gathered at the bottom in a perfect acoustical setting.

And the group played. It was soul-filling and lovely. And Clovis's flute trilled and wound around, and the tones danced and played through the music. At one time, all the others silenced their instruments and allowed Clovis's flute to be singly there. It was an acknowledgment of her skill; a salute. And Sling smiled.

With the first hint of rain, the violins fled. Then other musicians left, folding up their chairs and silently stealing away. Some of the cowards in the audience sneaked away, but the great majority stayed. And as the misting became a sprinkling, they raised their faces to it and laughed.

But the sky got darker and the rain became fairly steady. Finally they all trudged back in the instant mud, calling thanks and goodbyes, and they drove away.

Ethel said, "Since the roof leaks, why don't we take Miss Penny over to our place for now? Would you come, too?"

"Oh, no. I'll be fine. How kind of you to take Miss Penny."

Fredricka said, "I'll stay and help clear away the last of it."

Clovis exclaimed. "It's all done! I've never seen such good help. You were all just great, but Fredricka, you're a jewel."

"Of course."

Clovis smiled and waved them off.

Standing on the porch in the dripping rain, Sling said, "Come to my place."

"Don't be so rash."

"You can't stay here all by yourself."

Clovis scoffed. "The Creature of the Black Lagoon has been waiting for Miss Penny to leave?"

He watched her soberly. "I don't like you being here alone. I'll stay."

"No. You will not. Scoot. I'm exhausted." She was also beginning to get wet.

His Stetson protected him. "You know," he said earnestly, delaying, "I could have done better by Lizzie. I've watched Miss Penny today, and her life is entirely different here than it was at the Home. Lizzie could have had a wider acquaintance and done more things if I'd helped her more."

"You tried three companions for her whom she rejected. Her life was her own choice."

"Well. But she was under my jurisdiction. I should have seen to it that she got out more."

Clovis shrugged. "Everyone is responsible for his or her own life. You can't tell me that no one ever invited her anywhere. That would be impossible in this area. She must have refused so many times that people finally quit asking her. She had the freedom to do as she wanted. She was a leech."

"Well . . . yes. But I could have guided her better."

"You had all those kids and the other ladies to care about. Did Lizzie ever offer any help to you?"

"No."

It was a small word.

Clovis said, "You've been a good, busy, caring man in this community. I understand that it was you who brought the ballet to this area. That took some bravery in this macho world."

"These people weren't against the ballet, as such. They just didn't know how to go about getting it here. They are music devotees—you can surely understand that—and the ballet is what music looks like."

Clovis smiled at her love and complimented his word images. "Very good."

He looked at his woman silently for a long time before he said, "Without Lizzie, you'd never have come here."

"That is true."

"So, she did do something for me." Then he told Clovis, "The men are checking the herds and where they are to be sure they're okay if it really storms. We have to see if all the locks are down in the places we've made to store any water that comes our way. We didn't expect this. It could be rough. Will you be all right?"

"Of course."

"I could use a kiss."

She said, "I had one here somewhere."

She was searching in her pockets when he took hold of her, and she forgot what she was doing as he pulled her close and kissed her. It was a stunning act. She was overwhelmed.

So was he. He trembled with the need to control the force of his arms in holding her, so that he wouldn't crush her against him. Still, his embrace was not gentle, and his hungry mouth consumed hers.

He shuddered and gasped; then he said, "Come inside."

She had trouble just forming her lips, and he kissed her again. This was a lover's kiss—coaxing, influencing, inciting. His hands moved as he wanted, but with the sly and sneaky manner of a man who wanted his way.

In a growly, breathless voice, his body trembling and his hands shaking, he coaxed, "Come inside."

She put her forehead on his chest and said an uncertain, "No." Then she tilted back her head and said, "You have to see to the cattle and that the locks are closed in case the rain puddles."

And he was torn. For a Texan to have to choose between a woman and the possibility of stored water was a terrible thing. His slight, almost-nothing movements were jerky. He gasped air as if he would protest. He frowned and almost shook his head in tiny objections. And he tightened his mouth as he began to let her go. A woman can be had another time, but rain doesn't come that often. "I'll be back."

"No. You must not. It was bad enough that you sat with us in church. If you come back here while Miss Penny is away, it will look bad for me. You must not."

"Are you saying you don't want to be with me?"

He knew better than that. She watched him with bleak eyes. And she didn't reply.

"I'll be back."

"I'll set Spots on you."

He laughed, went off the wet porch and down the thirsty, sun-dried boards of the steps. His pickup was the last stranger's vehicle there. He got in and tooted his horn. She lifted a hand, and he drove away.

She called to Spots. But he was contented to watch from under the house. So, a little bedraggled from the day and the faltering rain, she drooped into the house. She went up the stairs and looked around at the ceilings, trying to consider where the last leaks had been. She set some buckets. Then she got her Yankee slicker and went up onto the roof.

In the last of the day's light, the gray of the mist veils was gorgeous. The subtle colors of the weeds and leaves, the dirt and wood were washed clean, and it was beautiful. She breathed deeply the smell of the fresh rain and filled her eyes with the beauty that lay beyond her roof.

She lifted her face to the mist and she heard the thunder was closer. It shook the ground, and she felt it through the boards of the house. She turned and frowned to the east. The clouds were heavier and restless looking.

Clovis went downstairs and turned on the weather station. There was an inert pocket of nothing that would not stop the storm. There were spin-off tornadoes, and the whole of Louisiana was under the storm watch. People were told to be alert—there could be flooding.

A little bit of Texas could be included in the storm's path. The whole northeastern part of Texas was alert to rain and the chance of high winds.

Clovis went up to the roof again and looked off toward the wash. If it really, really rained... It was pelting in blatting sounds, running down the slanted shade boards and dripping onto the tarped roof. She looked to the east and saw that the roiling storm clouds were not limited to the east; they were all around. Lightning was jagged in the sky and the house shook with the power resulting from the thunder crashes.

The electricity went off.

Clovis went out and firmly demanded Spots come into the house. He was a yard dog and he was embarrassed to be inside. He sat and looked, stretching his neck to see farther without moving. It took him some long time to relax.

But then as the night deepened, the fury of the storm increased.

The dog would start at the crashes of closer thunder and flinch at the lightning flashes that covered the whole universe with each bolt. The winds mounted to shrill pitches. It was almost intimidating.

Clovis was impressed with that. The dog didn't much like the storm, but he wasn't cowed by it. What a brave dog he was.

On the other hand, Clovis shivered with each crack of a lightning whip. She didn't like being on the first floor, and coaxed the dog upstairs.

The ensuing roar was greater than that of any wind she'd ever heard. It mounted to such an ungodly sound that Clovis crawled across the floor to the dog, and that was what saved her life.

The house was whipped around as if a humongous dog shook a house-size rat. The only thing that saved the house from being flung, God only knew where, was the surrounding, immovable grid of telephone poles and secure crossbeams.

The center post of the house gave way and the house was pressed against the front northeast corner of the pole barrier. The house buckled and tilted, windows burst and furniture was thrown around inside the strobe-lightning illuminated house.

In dead dark, the dying shrieks and groans of the house, the blows of furniture hitting the walls and the crashes of broken whatever made the whole thing a nightmare.

The rains came in brief torrents.

Since the possibility of any collectible rain was on the eastern part of his land, Sling and the hands had started with the closest gates. Checking them to be sure they were in place, and moving the cattle, they went up-country in the zigzag undulations of the land along the pockets they wanted filled. They were quite some distance from the house where Clovis was trapped. And it was by then on toward morning.

It was a dangerous night of storms, and the lightning was quirky. Without rain, in a single tree or in the close-packed herds, dry lightning could dance in the St. Elmo's fire of the sea. It was blue and spooky. But in a storm like this one, the white lightning bolts could kill. The men were careful to stay apart.

They heard the roar of wind and Tom heard Sling mutter, "Clovis." Sling raised up and stared off to the east. He was very tense for a while, then he relaxed. But he was terse and hurrying to get things done more quickly.

Peter said, "This is too fast a pace. Slow down."

Sling looked at Peter and frowned, then focused and saw him. "What?"

It was Peter who urged, "Why don't you go to her? We can get this done without you."

"I don't like not doing my share."

"You always do your share," Tom scolded. "We wear ourselves out trying to keep up with you. Go see if she's okay. Go on. We'll be all right."

"I know. I know. If she's all right, I'll be back."

"Don't be stupid. Stay there. We're almost through."

Sling said, "Yeah. Thanks. Be careful of yourselves."

Peter grumbled, "You had the care of your brothers for too long. We're grown men."

"Yeah." Sling got on Tucker and took off.

Peter yelled, "Slow down or you're liable to hurt the horse!"

And Sling slowed down.

Tom said to Pedro, "I hope I'm never that taken with a woman."

"She's a lady."

"Right."

It was just at dawn when Sling got to the house. He saw her on the roof as he came over the top of the dividing rise. She was there. Then he realized the house was wrecked. It was tilted and caved in. The beams of the shade were higher from the sloped roof. She had her red petticoat over the side.

She saw him coming and stood quietly watching him. He was every woman's dream.

As he came near, he talked Tucker closer to the house. He looked at her again, and she smiled at him. He stopped the horse about fifteen feet away and sat there, assimilating the fact that she was alive in that mess of a crushed tinderbox of dead wood. Very gently, he asked, "Decide to go down with the ship?"

She shook her head. "I have my red petticoat out."

"I'm here."

"I don't know how you're going to get us out of here. The stair is crumbled. It fell just after we—"

"'We'?"

"Spots is here."

"Ah."

"He's kept the snakes at bay."

"My God."

"It's been ... an ... interesting night."

"My love, I'll get you out of there."

"Actually, with the door closed, we're quite safe up here. Could you go for help? The phone went out about the same time the lights gave up."

"It was a tornado."

"I think you loosened the house when you tried to pull it down."

"My God."

"Oh, Sling, don't be silly. This old house was held together by my imagination. It was doomed by the first little wind that came along."

"I couldn't pull it down with my truck."

"You should have started with the top, not the bottom. The wind wasn't even of the main part of the tornado. If you will look, the path is over there." She pointed toward the wash.

"I'll see later." He undid his rope. "Get back, honey, I need to toss this up there."

"How can I help?"

"Don't worry, I'll get it."

And he did, with the first try. He looped the rope over the end of one of the slanting boards and pulled it tight. Then, with Tucker behaving perfectly and standing steady, Sling stood up on the saddle; and he held to the rope, hand over hand, as he walked up the side of what was left of the house.

When he got to the rail, he saw the tearstains on her face. Alone there, that strong, serene woman had wept. He stepped over the rail and secured the rope. He went to her and held her. Then she cried. And he soothed her and petted her, and his own eyes teared.

Spots paced around, trying for a little attention. But it was a while before Sling finally loosened a hand and leaned down to tell the dog he'd done a good job.

Sling put the rope around Spots and lowered the dog, freeing him just before he touched ground. It was a practiced move, so Clovis knew they'd done it before. The dog went over to where Tucker stood and they touched noses.

Then Sling went down the rope to Tucker and got another rope. He tied it to the saddle horn, went back up onto the roof and had Tucker back away from the house until the slant of the rope was correct. Then Sling fashioned a rope loop with the knot resting on top of the slanted rope. The seat was controlled by Sling's braking rope.

Then Sling sat Clovis in the loop and eased her over the rail, with her clutching that red petticoat as she held to the sides of the loop. He allowed her to slide down the rope to Tucker. The horse stood firm, and Clovis squirmed out of the seat and stepped down. Then she walked over to stand beside the dog.

Sling came down the side of the house using the braking rope.

The chicken pen was untouched. And the occupants were really quite well adjusted to their new home. Since their feathers were dry, they had to have taken shelter inside the unique house.

Sling went over to the now tilted back porch and wrested the feed drum upright. He scooped out enough feed for the chickens and carried it over to the pen.

Then he mounted Tucker, rode the few steps to Clovis and leaned over to pick her up, one-armed, and set her behind him.

She looked back. "My car is a mess."

"You'd be surprised how well it'll clean up."

"Where are we going?" she asked, her arms around his body, her cheek against his back.

"To my house."

"Oh."

He sighed. "I suppose you'll have to marry me, now that I'll have shot your reputation all to hell."

"I'm sure the ladies will consider the circumstances."

"Well, damn," he said with faked disgust. "That means I'll have to get you pregnant right away."

"Uhhh..."

"Don't give me any trouble," he warned. "You know darned good and well that you love me. I know it. How come you keep resisting the knowing?"

"I know it."

He asked, "Then what's the trouble?"

"Your commitment."

"You got it."

"Willingly?"

"Hell, woman, I was lost the minute you got out of your car."

"Then!"

"Yeah." He sighed. "I sure did a fine job of resisting. You've got to appreciate that fact. Do you know what I did?"

"What?"

And he gave her the gift of confessing his interest in her. "I pried off the slotted cover of the attic window and watched you with the telescope."

She hugged his back.

"And I forgot to put it back and a whole bunch of birds got in and everyone was running around shooing birds out of the—"

She laughed out loud.

"We went upstairs to see if any were left up there, and Chin had moved the telescope back to the other side of the attic. Do you know he's never mentioned doing that? So only he knows I was the one who left the opening uncovered and let the birds in...and why."

"I love you."

"Thank God for that. And you'll marry me?"

"Yes." She nuzzled her cheek against his back and hugged him.

He sighed. "I'm surely glad." He held her hands close against his chest.

They went to his house and he slid her down to watch as he stripped the saddle off Tucker and gave him a sugar cube. He saw to it that Spots got something to eat. Then he took her to the house.

There he let her have a shower. He got in and helped with that—being a good host, he said. Then he dried her with exquisite care and attention before he took her to his bed and made sure she really understood what was expected of her. He did start that sassily, but he got serious very soon.

"You do know how much I love you? You're a miracle. Do you understand that? I'll probably bless that damned Lizzie with every breath I take, all the rest of my life."

"You read what she wrote. You're a good man."

"And you love me."

"Oh, Sling, I do love you so much."

"You're the sweetest thing that has ever happened to me in all my life. I didn't know that I would find you. How many kids are we going to have?"

"I thought you didn't want to be bothered with kids and marriage."

"Well, I do find that I'm curious about what your babies will be like. And I like the idea of giving them to you."

"Do you, now?"

"Ummm. You are so beautiful. I'm so glad you don't have any clothes here. You can just run around naked. I'll like that. I like this, too." He put his hand on her here and there. His touch was sweet and loving. His mouth followed all his explorations, and he had her gasping.

Her breasts seemed to fill tautly and her legs became restless. Her mouth wanted his kisses, and deep in her body was a need that made her shiver in tremors of desire. She made hungry little noises and moved against him.

"You want something?" His voice was husky and soft.

"You."

"Well, that is something I'd be willing to help with. Here, let me arrange you just a little. My, but you are a beauty. Ummm, that's sweet. I like you doing that. Careful. Ahhh. Now, let me just... That's the way. Yes. And—"

"Oh, Ssslinnng."

"Honey, careful now. Uhhh. Ohhh. Don't do that yet. Wait a mmm..."

"Ummm?"

"You're a wicked, wicked woman!"

And she laughed a throaty laugh that made prickles run all over him and stood everything on end... like always.

It was several days before everything was cleaned up and organized. All the basins Sling had hoped would get a little water did have some.

The chickens were moved over to the Mueller place—tacky henhouse, fence and all—and the branded furniture was salvaged. But the old grandparents' house was demolished. The wood was chopped and sawed and stacked for winter nights and summer cookouts.

The contrived shade was left standing. She asked why, and he said, "We'll think of something."

Miss Penny made the move to the Mueller house in good spirits. But Clovis didn't have as much time for her then. She and Sling didn't notice that Miss Penny was a little lonely, but Chin did. So in order to get her out of Chin's kitchen, they had to get Miss Penny's old friend Miz Tooey from the Home.

And so the lovers were married. It was the event of that season because everybody showed up. There were the usual sly comments, the usual quarrels and the expected hilarity. It was very nice.

But it was late when Sling smiled at Clovis as they lay in their marriage bed. "Ahhh, Miz Mueller, I like having you in my arms. I like having you in my house. You know, I was lonely here without a family. It's nice to have people around again. But it's especially wondrous to have you in my bed. I am a contented man."

She rubbed his hairy stomach and said, "Really? It seems to me that you aren't completely so."

"I will be in an hour."

But it didn't take that long.

After several days had passed, Sling took the time to go to the Mueller cemetery. He put flowers on his parents' grave and told them his life was getting pretty near to perfect. And he told them he was beginning to understand why they'd needed to get off to themselves. He wanted them to know he no longer blamed them for their own deaths. He just wished they were around so they could know his new wife.

And then Sling went to the county cemetery and covered Lizzie's grave with yellow roses.

* * * * *

Bestselling author **NORA ROBERTS** captures all the
romance, adventure, passion and excitement of Silhouette in
a special miniseries.

THE CALHOUN WOMEN

Four charming, beautiful and fiercely independent
sisters set out on a search for a missing family
heirloom—an emerald necklace—and each finds
something even more precious... passionate romance.

Look for THE CALHOUN WOMEN miniseries
starting in June.

COURTING CATHERINE
Silhouette Romance #801

July
A MAN FOR AMANDA
Silhouette Desire #649

August
FOR THE LOVE OF LILAH
Silhouette Special Edition #685

September
SUZANNA'S SURRENDER
Silhouette Intimate Moments #397

CALWOM-1

 *Silhouette Books*®

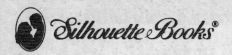 *Silhouette Books*®

SILHOUETTE BOOKS ARE NOW AVAILABLE IN STORES AT THESE CONVENIENT TIMES EACH MONTH*

Silhouette Desire and Silhouette Romance

> May titles: April 10
> June titles: May 8
> July titles: June 5
> August titles: July 10

Silhouette Intimate Moments and Silhouette Special Edition

> May titles: April 24
> June titles: May 22
> July titles: June 19
> August titles: July 24

We hope this new schedule is convenient for you. With only two trips each month to your local bookseller, you will always be sure not to miss any of your favorite authors!

Happy reading!

Please note: There may be slight variations in on-sale dates in your area due to differences in shipping and handling.

*Applicable to U.S. only.

SDATES-RR

Take 4 bestselling love stories FREE

Plus get a FREE surprise gift!